The small, barefoot African and the large Englishman, bags under his eyes, bags in his trousers, his paunch-tightened shirt bursting over his belt, left the workshop arm in arm, and walked down the driveway to a waiting Mercedes with *Department of Technical Assistance* written on the door. Before the Englishman got into the car he stopped, looked up the driveway to Sam Fong, winked, and erected his thumb in what he intended as a gesture of mutual triumph. Sam Fong raised a ripe middle finger to the man, something he had not done since he was a very young boy in Central China.

*Also by Paul Theroux:*

FICTION

*Waldo**
*Girls at Play*
*Jungle Lovers*
*Sinning with Annie*
*Saint Jack*
*The Black House*
*The Family Arsenal*
*The Consul's File*
*A Christmas Card*
*Picture Palace*
*London Snow*
*World's End*
*The Mosquito Coast*
*The London Embassy*
*Half Moon Street*
*O-Zone**
*My Secret History*

CRITICISM

*V. S. Naipaul*

NONFICTION

*The Great Railway Bazaar*
*The Old Patagonian Express*
*The Kingdom by the Sea*
*Sailing Through China*
*Sunrise with Seamonsters*
*The Imperial Way*
*Riding the Iron Rooster**

*Published by Ivy Books

# FONG
# AND THE
# INDIANS

# Paul Theroux

IVY BOOKS • NEW YORK

*For Anne*

"...*The entry of the Asiatic as labourer, trader, and capitalist into competition in industry and enterprise not only with, but in, the Western world is a new fact of first importance*..."

—Winston Churchill,
*My African Journey*,
1908.

# Author's Note

I WOULD LIKE TO SET THE RECORD STRAIGHT ON A FEW DE-
tails. In Kenya, there is an Uhuru Avenue, but I have never
seen any Chinese grocery stores on it. Sam Fong and his store
are made up. I have also given the impression in this book that
East Africa is one country. It is not; it is actually an area
which comprises three countries, Kenya, Uganda and Tanzania, each with its own kind of porridge, politics, currency
and army. These countries have common services and the
presidents often meet in one of the three capitals to clink
glasses and toast unity, but the East African Federation no
longer exists.

There are roughly 400,000 "Asians" (that is, people of
Indo-Pakistani origin) who consider East Africa their home.
The majority of Africans feel differently; they often say it is
time for the Asians to leave, and sometimes they deport them.
There are Asians in Kenya, Uganda and Tanzania whose
names are Patel, Gupta, Fakhru, etc., but these names are as
common as Smith and Jones in the United States. The Patels
fill four pages in the Kenya telephone directory, for example,
and it is not a very big directory.

I could not have written this book without many useful
conversations with my friend and guru, Rashmi Desai.

PAUL THEROUX

Kampala, Uganda

# PART ONE

# 1

THE GROCERY STORE ON UHURU AVENUE (FORMERLY Queensway) was owned by Sam Fong, a Chinese immigrant. They called him an immigrant; actually he had lived in East Africa longer than the Prime Minister, who was an African. But to be one Chinaman in a country of seven million Africans is not easy: you stand out; the East cannot save you; you remain a visible immigrant all your born days and so do your children, and so do theirs.

On the window of the store in white irregular letters was written FRIEND FROCERY POP IN PLEASE FOR BETTER PRICE ANYWHERE IN AFRICA. Some Swahili progress slogans had been written on the window but were now scratched out. Four years after Independence Sam Fong discovered that the less said about progress the better. The slogans antagonized his customers and often got him into ideological hot water. Take ONE MAN, ONE VOTE (a stick figure with a ballot between its fingers illustrated this slogan). Many Africans came into the grocery

3

store and said, "Big words, big vote. Where this thing vote? You tell me."

"Like the Holy Spirit"—Fong was a Catholic—"the vote is everywhere. But you can't see it, that's all," said Fong, grinning and thinking how much better the sentence would have sounded in Chinese than Swahili.

"These bloody fool politicians," the African would answer. "There is no vote, just their fat asses in big cars forever. Finish, that's all. Give me the British any day. At least they don't talk through their ass. Those British they say what they mean. If they think you bloody baboon they say straight out, 'I think you African chaps are bloody baboon.' British are too honest, you know. That's why everyone like them *kabisa*. But these politicians are bloody sheet."

"Be patient," Fong would say. This he had been saying nearly every day of his thirty-five years in East Africa. When he realized that the progress slogans upset his African customers he scratched them off the window.

In spite of the fact that many of Fong's white customers might say (and often did say), "The Chinese are born grocers," Sam Fong was not a born grocer. It should have been clear to anyone standing in the grocery store that Fong's real genius was in carpentry: the hardwood shelves covered every wall from floor to ceiling; bins, vats, counters, stools— all mortised and tenoned (not a nail in the place)—were everywhere, unbreakable, sturdy, hard, with chamfered edges and smooth surfaces. But on the formidable expanse of shelves were only a few cans, a few lonely packages of tea and hair straightener and skin lightener. On the smooth counter, as big as the Congo, was a tin receptacle containing stale bread and a few old cream buns; in the bins some onions were starting to shoot green stalks into each other; in the vats maybe a dozen handfuls of rice. Speaking plainly, there were no groceries in the grocery store. The only piece of grocery store furniture that appeared to be fulfilling its design and justifying its labor was the stool Sam Fong's wife Soo sat on, week after week, smiling at the empty shelves beyond.

Sam Fong *had* been a carpenter. The grocery store came

after Independence when necessity forced Fong to learn a new profession. He had been a foreman in the carpentry shop of the Ministry of Works when East Africa was a British Protectorate. Shortly after Independence an Englishman came up to Fong and asked, "In point of fact, I want you to tell me straight out, Fong, who would you say is the keenest chap in the workshop? I don't want a dogsbody, you understand." The Englishman bared his teeth. "I want someone terribly keen."

Sam Fong thought a moment and then pointed to Mohinder Singh, chief *fundi* of the workshop; Singh was gnawing a dowel that he found too large for a hole.

"No, no, not a *muhindi*. I want a native, an African chap, you see? A black one."

"Take anyone," said Sam Fong.

"Are they all that keen?"

"No. They're all the same. Useless buggers," said Sam Fong in Swahili. "Buggers" he said in English.

"I'm afraid I can't agree with you there, Fong. No sir, I can't. You give these people half a chance and there's no telling what will happen. Oh, I know, we're not in charge anymore, but that's hard cheese; we'll just have to live with it. Now for goodness sake, Fong, point me out a keen chap. I'm a busy man."

Fong shrugged in the direction of an African man in rags sawing a board. The man sawed very quickly with one hand and picked his teeth with the other hand. The board was held firm by the man's toes which curled round the edges and prevented it from moving. "Keen chap," said Fong, "like the rest of them." These words were Sam Fong's undoing.

The next day the Englishman appeared again and handed the African an envelope. The African, who was working on his back under a table at the time, glanced over and took the envelope firmly between the large and second toe of his right foot.

Sam Fong looked on in horror. He half expected the African to rip open the envelope with his toes and hold up the letter with his left foot for all to see. The African did not do this. Instead, he just raised his right foot a few inches, holding the envelope above the sawdust, the wood shavings and spittings, and continued drilling the hole under the table. Neither the Englishman, nor Sam Fong, nor the envelope moved for a full five minutes. The African put down his drill and moved out from under the large table sideways, like a crab. He passed the envelope from his foot to his left hand, and, squatting on the floor, opened it. He looked at the Englishman.

The Englishman's face brightened and twisted itself into a smile so large that it was almost not a smile; the Englishman's eyes popped and he clasped his hands behind his back and rocked on his heels. He turned his face to Sam Fong and continued rocking and grinning, although Fong remained horror-struck, yellow, his eyes and mouth only slits in a lineless face.

The African looked bewildered, almost harmed. He walked up to the Englishman and said softly, "I'm going to England."

"You deserve it, son," said the Englishman, bouncing once on his toes. "You're a keen chap."

The African went over to Sam Fong. "I'm going to England," he said.

"May your misbegotten children die diseased in a whorehouse there. I hope you never come back," said Sam Fong in Chinese. He grinned and then uttered a Swahili proverb.

The small, barefoot African and the large Englishman, bags under his eyes, bags in his trousers, his paunch-tightened shirt bursting over his belt, left the workshop arm in arm, and walked down the driveway to a waiting Mercedes with *Department of Technical Assistance* written on the door. Before the Englishman got into the car he stopped, looked up the driveway to Sam Fong, winked, and erected his thumb in what he intended as a gesture of mutual triumph. Sam Fong raised a ripe middle finger to the man, something he had not done since he was a very young boy in central China.

Sam Fong's curse was not as powerful as the will of the Department of Technical Assistance. The African came back six months later. He had gone on a carpentry course in Birmingham where he found out about drill presses, steam drills and table saws that could do the work of ten men. If Fong had been in the habit of going to the movies he might have seen, in "News from Britain," the face of the African he cursed being shown around the Birmingham Technical School by a man in a white smock. Looking on were two Nigerians, a Zambian, a Ghanaian in a robe, a Sudanese in a fez and a Kenyan in a three-piece suit carrying a fly whisk which he flicked at giant whirring machines. Sam Fong's keen chap was wearing real clothes and even a pair of shoes, and later in the film operated a drill press while the six Africans and twenty white Birmingham Tech students applauded and waved into the camera. At the end of the film, while the narrator said, " . . . but it's not all work and no play for these keen carpenters . . ." the Africans were shown riding a red double-decker bus, eating a meal of fish and chips topped off with large helpings of jellied eels, being shown what looked like a museum by a bald man with a thick gold chain around his neck, and (" . . . there was lots of merriment in store for these keen craftsmen in wood . . .") dancing with large-chinned and flat-chested English girls from "right across the Highroad at Birmingham Domestic Science College where five Zanzibaris will finish their course this year."

When Mohinder Singh came to work the next morning and described "News from Britain" to Sam Fong (" . . . dancing with a *muzungu* girl and goodness knows what . . ."), Sam Fong wept. His tears were scarcely dry when the African showed up and announced, with an official letter of appointment as proof, that he was foreman. Fong was given a drill. He handed his pencil and clipboard to the African and, cursing in Chinese, took his place under the half-made furniture, on his back, "like a whore in Shanghai," he reflected.

The African now wore suits, bought a motorcycle and a fountain pen and carried a humming transistor radio with him wherever he went; he showed up to work late and drunk, called the other Africans bloody baboons and useless natives and began saying to Sam Fong, "Carry on then . . . I'll leave you to get on with it . . . Pull your finger out . . . Belt up or I'll sack you off . . ." One day, about a month after Fong gave up his clipboard, the African foreman said, "Carry on, you bugger, or I'll buy one of those super drills that does do the work of ten fat men!"

Sam Fong sighed. "What do you want, *bwana*?"

"I am asking you are you knowing what the drill is this side?"

"This is the drill," said Fong holding up his drill.

"Are you being cheeky with me?" asked the foreman angrily. "I can have your bloody job if you act *kali* . . ."

Sam Fong stood up, brushed off the wood shavings, looked at the foreman, said "You belong in a tall tree" in Chinese and then "*Kwaheri*, bye-bye." He mounted his bicycle and pedaled quickly out of the Ministry of Works compound, away from the Work for Progress posters and the shrieks of the foreman who was attempting to disperse the crowd of workmen that had gathered.

Sam Fong never went back. On the way home he made three resolutions: never trust a white, never trust a black, never be a carpenter; as he repeated these resolutions to himself he saw a sign reading STORE FOR HIRE APLY FAKHRU ENTERPRISES LTD., and later that afternoon signed a ten-year lease with a pajama-clad Ismaili who demanded fifty pounds in advance for a moldering empty shop at the lower end of Uhuru Avenue. In the contract was a clause which read, "And I promise to buy all stocks and stores and goods from the above-named Hassanali Fakhru at prices to be agreed upon so help me God." Only later, in the heat of argument was this pointed out to Fong. The lumber for the shelves and counters, the bins, the vats, the scales, the light bulbs, the plate glass, were also bought, again under protest, from Fakhru. Twice a day, in Chinese and Swahili, Sam Fong said to Fakhru, "I hate you, I hate you . . . You're a blood-sucking Indian, and if you did this in China the Emperor would cut your tongue out, your hands off and he would wisely make your penis into sausage for the dogs!"

Hassanali Fakhru listened to the jerky Swahili, smiled and answered, "The trouble with you foreigners is you're not interested in building a nation. You have no spirit of *harambee*.

You just make money and then go back where you came from and leave our poor African brothers with nothing. Now me, I can tell you I am interested in developing this country and building a multiracial society and I have to deal with shit like your kind to do so. The contract was finalized long ago so there's no need crying over spilt milk. Buggers like you make my job very hard, let me remind you, and give Asia a bad name. Now piss off, my friend."

Sam Fong would utter a vile Chinese oath and make his way, past hand-colored portraits of the Aga Khan with a garland around his neck, to the door. With a belch, and smoothing his pajama top, Fakhru would return to his papers. It happened twice a day. There was no need, he felt, for either party to get excited; such was business. During these first six months Sam Fong worked on his shelves, and even taking into consideration the tyranny of Fakhru, Fong considered the six months to be very happy ones. He worked all day and far into the night sawing and sanding and banging pegs into the shelves and counters; he did not have to draw plans. He had a good eye and could measure anything by merely looking at it. He was foreman, workman and customer. He was alone in his work and very happy with his tools and wood. He worked steadily, and the shelves in the shop in his mind soon became the shelves in Fakhru's hired *duka*. They were lovely large shelves, very strong and smooth, braced and solid. Fong knew they were beautiful, but still he remembered his resolutions and refused to do any carpentry for anyone but himself. He vowed never to allow himself the humiliation of being an employee ("Get on with the job or I'll sack you off!") or even a confidant ("Tell me, Fong, who's the keenest chap in the workshop?").

As the weeks passed he grew more and more worried about the prospect of becoming a grocer, while still resolved that he would never be a carpenter again. Being a grocer frightened him, opening his own store frightened him, and soon all this fear transformed itself into rage at night and he started beating his wife to calm himself. His wife, Soo, understood and received each beating on good faith. It was just another wifely

burden. Many times she had to remind herself of her obligation to shriek.

Two days before the opening Soo stayed in the shop and
busied herself with white paint and a large board. At the end
of the day she showed Fong the sign: FRIEND FROCERY POP IN
PLEASE FOR BETTER PRICE ANYWHERE IN AFRICA. She smiled.
"This is your sign. This is your store, noble husband. You are
now a grocerman," she said in Chinese. Instead of being
pleased Sam Fong felt only fear, and for her sign and her
words Soo Fong was so severely beaten that she was unable to
attend the Grand Opening.

"I am abundantly heppy—overjoyed I should say—to be
the honored patron of this Grand Opening Day of the Sam
Fong grocery *duka*," Fakhru said to his brother-in-law, Sam
Fong and the five African stragglers who had caught sight of
the ribbon across the door of the grocery. Fakhru's speech,
written by his son who had been directed, "Big words in this
or I'll kick your ass to Zanzibar," took well over thirty minutes to deliver. Fong agreed to the speech only because his
own English was faulty; in fact, his entire English vocabulary
consisted of nouns for food and perhaps ten verbs which he
always used in the present continuous tense. He felt humiliated and helpless; his bitter enemy and master, Hassanali
Fakhru, stood in the doorway and spoke. But it was only
temporary, an hour at most and then he would be free.

Fakhru referred to Sam Fong's perseverance and high
values, Asian values, tried and true. He went on to speak at
length of how he, Fakhru, had started out from just such humble beginnings. He spoke of the necessity for lifting oneself up
into the world by one's own bootstraps. Snatches of the
Koran, progress slogans and parts of pop songs ("As our
friends the Beatles say, money cannot buy us love . . .") were
also part of the speech, and he finished by saying, "I do believe I have covered up all the major points . . ."

Soon it came time to cut the ribbon. Sam Fong held out a
pair of Mother's Own Cutting Scissors (Fakhru Enterprises
Ltd., four shillings, sixpence), and Fakhru and Fong, each
with his thumb in a metal loop, began sawing away at the

ribbon. The leverage was wrong and instead of the blades
working against each other they were far apart. A good minute
passed and the ribbon was not even frayed. Fakhru lost his
temper, pulled Fong's thumb out of the loop and threw the
scissors down. Then he lifted the ribbon, and chomping down
once with betel-stained teeth, tore the ribbon in half. "That's
how we do such things where I come from," said Fakhru,
holding the two ends of the ribbon. His brother-in-law
snapped a picture.

Sam Fong stood impassive and stiff. The people on the
sidewalk clapped and then went away. Off in the distance Soo
moaned.

"And now for the Grand Opening," said Fakhru. "I shall be
your first customer."

The two men entered the store. Except for the carefully
made furnishings the store was almost bare. Sam Fong went
behind the counter and folded his arms.

"If you please, kind sir," said Fakhru showing his teeth, "I
would like a becket of tea."

"Big-big or small-small?" inquired Fong, now leaning on
the counter gingerly in the manner of a grocer.

"Bit smaller," said Fakhru.

Fong went to a corner of the store where on a large shelf
sat a tiny box of tea. He placed the box of tea in front of
Fakhru.

"You see," said Fakhru, "it's not that I am not liking tea.
I'm crazy for tea. But I am having lots of tea beckets already.
I just want to be your first customer. I'll take it."

"Two shillings, only," said Fong.

Fakhru slapped his fat palm against his wide perspiring
forehead and made a meaty *plop*. "You said *two shillings*?"

"Right. Now I grocery man, you customer. You pay, I take
money."

"You buy this goods from me for sixpence, you sell to me
for two shillings. You call that business?"

"What you calling it?"

"When I have to pay you one shilling sixpence to be first

customer I rather be second customer and save money. I call it robbery."

"You stealing from me, I stealing from you. That business," said Fong.

"I give you ninepence only. If you refuse I give you broken arm quick," said Fakhru, throwing two coins on the counter. "That the thanks I get for being first customer."

Fakhru spat a long stream of betel juice through the notch in his front teeth. The juice landed on the floor like a red bubbly snake, a bad omen suddenly materializing out of thin air. Clutching his tiny box of tea in his hand he stormed out of the shop with a swish and flap of his large pajama trousers. His jaw was moving back and forth rapidly, kneading his betel for another go.

With Fakhru gone the shop was in silence. The two Grand Opening ribbons fluttered when Fakhru brushed by, but now hung limp. Sam Fong stared past the empty door. From the woodwork came a slow wail: Soo in pain several rooms away. Fong dropped the two coins into a wooden box, leaned against the counter, took a deep breath, sighed, and four years passed.

# 2

THERE WERE THREE MORE CHILDREN NOW, AND NONE SEEMED larger than a frog; the older children—two of them—would have helped their father, but there was nothing for them to do.

In four years all that Sam Fong had managed to do was to perfect a tight grin which he was able to switch on and off. He had never grinned so much in his life. As a carpenter he did not have to grin at all. As a grocer he found that he spent most of the day grinning. He would not have noticed it except that it made his face hurt, and it was only much later (perhaps two years) that he could grin painlessly. On the other hand, his wife, who had very large teeth, found it a great relief to grin. All of this, Fong reflected, was business.

The carpenter in Fong did not die. Fong continued to hammer, saw and plane; when the counter got very dirty or the shelves very greasy it was the carpenter and not the grocer in Sam Fong that took charge. Instead of washing the counter he sanded it down; if there was a lot of grease on the counter it was planed. When a feeble African woman dropped a whole bottle of vinegar on the floor one day Fong rushed into the back room, grabbed his crowbar and hammer, tore up the floorboards and fitted new ones. After these carpentry exercises, done at top speed, Fong felt very well; it was a much better feeling than he got from beating his wife. Hammering helped him fight his moments of depression, though after four years—spent mostly leaning against the counter—Fong felt like throwing up the whole business and walking away. His moments of remorse over quitting the carpentry job were quickly dispelled, if not brightened, by the memory of the African at the Ministry of Works telling him to carry on, that keen chap who tormented the carpenters and who, if given a second chance, would make Fong's life miserable. Fong remembered his resolution and went back to hammering mindlessly on the counter; at other times he would go to see Fakhru and buy what Fakhru called "Stocks and Stores."

The largest selling items in the store were the five kinds of skin lightener (three for women, two for men). Sam Fong thought it was odd that there should be only one kind of bread, one kind of matches, one kind of cigarettes, one kind of ketchup and *five* kinds of skin lightener. He made up a joke which he told to everyone who bought a tube of the skin lightening cream: customer walks in; customer asks for skin lightener; Fong gets skin lightener and hands it to customer saying, "Now you be Chinese like me." No one thought it was funny. Once, when he asked an African what he was going to do with the cream, the African said it was good for the cold weather, it prevented lips from getting stiff and (this was the African's exact word) "unsightly." With each crate of skin lightener a poster was enclosed: Fong studied these carefully. There were always four characters in the picture—each a different dusky shade. Fong's favorite was the airplane poster. On this one the four people were deployed around the movable stairs for a just-arrived plane. A shiny purplish man oiled a tire, a man with a dull, carbonized face wiped the rail of the stairs, and both men looked blackly upon their shabby tasks; their coveralls were soiled with blotches of soot and finger-wipings of plane grease. Standing on the runway was a mocha air hostess greeting a prosperous quadroon-yellow African carrying an attaché case. A sizzling part had been burned across one temple, and a thought-bubble at the side of his head contained the following: "Boy! She sure is some dish! I am sure glad I bought that extra tube!"

This yellow African with a slightly oriental look about him stuck in Fong's mind and would not leave. And though none of his customers saw the humor in it, and went on believing privately that even a small tube of skin lightener could squirt them surely into the middle class (whiteness being the confessed aspiration of many of them), Sam Fong persisted with his joke: "Now you be Chinese like me."

When Fong went to buy "Stocks and Stores" from Fakhru he made up his mind that he would buy only the necessary items; inevitably he came back with much more than he wanted, though much less than he bargained for. On paper what he bought looked like a great deal; when it was delivered in the rattling, gray Peugeot van that bore Fakhru's name, it looked like very little. These sessions with Fakhru wore Fong down and caused Soo Fong many days in bed recovering from the bruises which the enraged and humiliated Sam Fong inflicted on her. The beatings were, as before, accepted by her with great forbearance; "welcomed" is perhaps the wrong word, though there was more than mere acceptance in her attitude toward the beatings, and often she was pleased in the knowledge that she was fulfilling a useful function. (There is more than a smattering of masochism in any folk culture.) In order for Fong to get what he wanted from Fakhru he had to agree to buy other things.

Fakhru had introduced Fong to the fascination of black market merchandise. "You know bleck market?" Fakhru had asked. Sam Fong stared. Fakhru translated into Swahili.

"Yes," said Fong. "In town."

"Where in town?" asked Fakhru.

"Where they sell the bananas," said Sam Fong.

Fakhru smiled and wiped his whole sweating face on his pajama front which he lifted with two hands. He spat. "Not *that* market. Now I tell you about real bleck market," he said.

He told him. But after two transactions in the Congo (one in Kinshasa, one in Lubumbashi) Fong was lost. He never understood why the border guards should be bribed; he never fully comprehended the smoked fish thrown on top of the merchandise, the exchange-control shell game in which the Congolese francs were converted into salt, then into ivory, then into cigarettes and finally, at some equatorial out-station, into shillings and at some future date (this last transaction known only to Fakhru) into rupees. Fong nodded. "Now I know black market."

Black market with its elaborate ritual of almost religious proportions, came to be synonymous with high quality and instant wealth. Sam Fong accumulated mattresses, yards and yards of Belgian cloth, galvanized pails and dozens of other items which no one bought, but which Fong thought useful to have around the store in case a customer should come into the store with more than a shilling. At the start of the bargain when Fakhru would mention an item Fong would recoil.

"Good recapped tires just arrived."

"Don't want tires," Fong would say. "I selling grocery food."

"Good recapped tires you don't want," Fakhru would say. "Sal right with me. Everybody wants those tires, those *bleck market tires*."

"You say *black market tires*?"

"That is what I did say."

And Fong would buy a dozen. Eventually he would sell three and the rest would be used in flower beds for planned but unfinished gardens; one hung by a rope would become a swing, others would be cut to pieces to be made into sandals.

With the exception of some tea, sugar, matches, rice, patent medicine ("Samson Blood-Purifying Lozenges," "Uncle Pompey's Gripe Water"), hair straightener and skin lightener, the goods that Fakhru fobbed off onto Sam Fong—and in particular, the black market goods—rarely sold. If they did, they yielded no profit. They were usually too big to be displayed, and so the store always seemed uniquely bare. Soo thought of taking down the grocery store sign every time Fong bought a new black market item. When he bought mattresses Soo imagined a new sign: SAM FONG MATTRESS SHOP; or the tires: SAM FONG TIRES FOR ALL OCCASIONS, but always he would sell a few and permit the rest to be transmogrified into sandals, flower pots, etc. The mattresses that were not sold were torn apart by a cripple who, for two shillings a mattress, made each spring into a coat hanger. The coat hangers did not sell either, but when Soo pointed this out to Sam Fong he replied, "Yes, I know, Africans don't want them: no coat, no coat hanger. But they're easy to store, no?"

A system was inevitable, it was the difference between life and death, and after four years Fong had worked it out in detail. He made lists of the things Africans bought and had a final list of high priority items: cigarettes sold singly, matches, blood-purifying lozenges, fruit salts, sugar, hair straightener, skin lightener, aspirin, kerosene, unrefined Nubian gin, tea and a few other things. The dust-covered canned goods he learned never to restock; they had been on the shelves since the Grand Opening Day. Among these were ten cans of Spam which had been packed in Austin, Minnesota; thirty-five cans of Australian processed cheese from Melbourne; and about a gross of cans with no label except the following scrap, sometimes studied by Fong, stuck to one of the crates: "The ruddy-bright delicious juice of fine tomatoes—excellent for any meal or as a between-meal refresher and a terrific source of Vitamins C and A ... [the next part was illegible, then] ... *Serving Suggestions* ... Serve chilled as a beverage; hot as a soup or beverage; or use it for making aspic salads, sauces, stews, etc. Drink it morning, noon or night ... *Quick 'n' Easy Appetizer or Snack Idea* ... With your favorite crackers add one 3-ounce package ..." The rest was torn. Sam Fong had stopped dusting the cans and had given up trying to fathom the writing on the crate. To open one of these label-less cans was to throw three shillings to the wind, for whatever was in cans Fong did not like. At first he had said to his customers, "Just arrived from Minn— nice good meat in very strong can," or

"Honest better price for this sent today by my brother in Australia... ," or (in the case of the gross of unmarked cans) "What is inside is secret—only three shillings to have secret revealed..." No one bought the cans; this ceased to worry Sam Fong and even pleased Soo Fong. No grocery store was complete, she felt, unless there were cans on the shelves. Empty shelves upset her. It is perhaps in the nature of every grocer to develop a weird anthropomorphism for groceries: Soo felt sorry for the tiny stack on the large shelves; to stare at a pyramid of three small boxes of tea, alone in a corner of the store, untouched, caused her genuine pain. She averted her eyes from the pathetic little piles of unsold merchandise in the grocery store.

Life went on. Somehow Fong managed a small profit, but nearly all of it was spent in rent, "Stocks and Stores" and overhead expenses. Some he put in the bank, but only as a gesture, for he never banked more than a few shillings. The last week of the month—the week before Soo took her abacus down from the shelf and began flinging the beads to and fro as her husband barked his cheek-tightening Chinese at her—was a terrible one: the tea was watered to a sickly urinous color, meat did not exist, no one used soap and grasshoppers caught under the streetlights at night and fried were the main course at every meal. The children sat in their corner of the back room and grumbled over their grasshoppers. Sam Fong would silence the complaints with: "Eat these nice fat insects. You are lucky to have them. In China they are a delicacy."

Often Fong regretted having made his resolution about never being a carpenter, but the resolution was irrevocable. The other two—never trust a white man, never trust a black man—also caused him considerable anxiety. His customers, when they appeared at their infrequent intervals, were either white or black. If a white man bought something (the whites never bought much more than cigarettes, but they always bought the whole package of twenty and never asked for only two or three), Fong felt he was being cheated or spied upon. Africans made him nervous as well and many were the times when an African in a clean shirt and tie, perhaps even wearing a suit, walked in and awakened fear in Fong, the helpless fright that envisioned the African announcing that he was the new owner of the grocery store and that Fong should pick up the bundle of papyrus and begin sweeping the floor. This, in four years, had not happened; but the anxiety, together with the knowledge that the Africans were in power and he himself was "free" (the image of a man splashing in a wide muddy river occurred to him), prompted another saying which he repeated incessantly to his wife: "A man who is free to feed himself might choose poison," and sometimes worded as "When people are free anything is possible, even tyranny." The African who, in six brief months, became foreman of the workshop also became the symbol of what Fong imagined would be inevitable frustration and eventual failure. He trusted no one except a fellow Chinaman who ran a camera shop and spoke of going to Canada. There were, he had heard, three other Chinese in the country, but he had never seen them. They lived in the bush. His dealings with whites inspired less anxiety than his dealings with Africans, but much more futility, for he was certain that the whites were responsible for his ended career in carpentry. His resolutions did not cover brown men; he continued to do business with Fakhru, and, with more rage than anxiety, more insolence than fear, get cheated. He knew he was being cheated by Fakhru and he explained this in another proverb: "Behind every dark man there is a white man making money." This became to his wife and him, crouched in the light of an oil lamp over their fried grasshoppers and urinous tea at midnight on the last week of the month, one of his wise sayings.

Fong was more worried about being cheated than he was about making money. Cheating made him squirm; it made him nervous and murderous. Making money was not one of his dreams. He did not sit in his store and dream about Nubians carrying trays of fried pork and jugs of rice wine, tall black men in silk wearing gold daggers and waiting on him, cooling him with feathery fans. He did not imagine himself sitting in the back seat of a Mercedes shouting for his driver to turn left, or, with the car radio blasting, drawing up to the Nile Villa Hotel while dozens of curious and greedy onlookers asked, "Who is that wealthy Chinaman?" and stared. These were Soo's dreams, two of them at any rate, and she stopped speaking of them to Fong when quite in earnest he beat her unmercifully for repeating them to him. He had explained to Soo that this was another world, her world of fantasy, and it was not populated with people like Sam or Soo Fong. The idea of wealth was not just unattainable, it was unthinkable; when the thought was uttered he ridiculed it. He was meant to serve, to work; and lately his preoccupation with being swindled prevented him from having time even to ridicule the thought of wealth.

Sometimes he thought of happiness. This idea of happiness was set among wood shavings in a noisy workshop. Table legs were being turned on a lathe, drills scraped against wood and bored into the center of thick boards, gouges turned up long curls on doors that would be graceful and muscular men pounded pegs into joints while Sam Fong, like the leader in a Chinese musical revue, directed the busy men with a little lemon branch, his nostrils full of sawdust. No one was paid, no one cheated and lovely smooth furniture bounced out of the workshop on short hard legs, like indestructible little men, sturdy and mindless. This could hardly be called the dream of a voluptuary, but this was Sam Fong's dream, based on his happiest days in Africa when there was no money and when he had plenty to eat. He had renounced it, but because he had renounced it as a way of life it became sacred to him; he would see it after death. The workshop in this other sphere was bathed in a rosy glow from the lumber room; each naked man acted on his command and was dwarfish and serene in his industry. Money had nothing to do with it, though cheating certainly did; he knew for the time being he had been cheated out of it all.

He narrowed his eyes at the empty shelves and sold an African a two-ounce tube of skin lightener and three cigarettes. Though the tube cost three shillings sixpence and the cigarettes tenpence, he took the African's twenty-shilling note, and, without blinking or moving his head, or even without looking at the man, gave him the exact change. On this day, more than four years after his shop was opened, Sam Fong became a *dukawallah*.

# 3

Sam Fong heard something inside his head rattling; it was like the loose bolt in an old ripsaw handle that only an unskilled carpenter could tolerate, someone who knew nothing about tools. He pressed the side of his head, as if that might tighten up the bolt. Nothing happened. The noise, *clank-clank*, continued. Fong looked toward the front of the store and saw that the real cause of the noise was not a loose bolt but rather a white man. The white man was picking up and dropping little cans on one of the shelves. The white man was also talking out of the side of his mouth to a man next to him who was not white, but not black either; and when Fong stared at him he realized that the man was not brown, and not yellow. Next to the white man the other man looked simply non-white, and this man listened intently to the white man who was still dropping the little cans on the shelf and talking in a language Fong had never heard before. The noise, the men, the foreign language caused Sam Fong's groin to ache and become very cold. For a moment Fong felt like killing both of the men, or, at the very least, beating his wife to a pulp.

Fong turned to Soo and shouted at her in Swahili.

Soo stared at him wonderingly, as if he had just struck her. She did not move; her intent gaze made her look as if she were leaning toward him softly. She was still a pretty woman. Even after eight children, many beatings, large helpings of grasshoppers and hard work she retained a definite facial beauty, and her hands were like small new plants. She had married at twelve and was now not much over thirty. The marriage had been arranged by mail. Bundles of twenty-shilling notes wrapped in a greasy letter written by the Chinaman in the camera store had been sent to Hong Kong, and from there to Soo's father. At first Fong thought he might have to go all the way back to Hong Kong or Shanghai to get her. But with the help of an Armenian rug merchant who was fleeing for his life and his millions, Soo's father put her on a ship and she was on her way to Mombasa with an envelope of rose petals, incense for the bridal bed and her maidenhead intact, before her twelfth birthday. Sam Fong took the train to Mombasa where he slept among cotton bales, dodged Arabs at night and sweltered during the day among foul-smelling Bajuni sailors; and one day the ship arrived. When he saw her, Fong was surprised by the smallness of the girl—no one had ever mentioned that she was twelve years old. Fong took her up-country on the train, through the bush and past the grassgrown volcanoes to his little hut on the equator, and once back, treated her like his daughter for one year. He bought her sweet cakes and bracelets, took her for walks, bought her cloth, sang her songs of boatmen and people playing in paddies among new blossoms; he held her gently and let her snore innocently against his chest, and at the end of the year, and the end of his vow to the quaint Chinese custom of waiting, and, needless to say, at the end of his wits he dragged Soo into his bedroom one noon, threw her on the bed and fell on top of her. It was like a huge farm implement plowing up one pale flower, not quite crushing it. Soo said nothing. Her face expressed only one emotion well: wonderment. And so when

Sam Fong screamed at her in Swahili she looked at him with every inch of her lovely lemon face showing wonderment.

"I am very sorry, dear husband and master," said Soo, "but I have not enough knowledge of this tongue to understand what you are saying." She spoke in Chinese.

Sam Fong nodded and captured a whiff of air in his mouth. He exhaled the following in Chinese: "You see those white men there playing with cans? Serve them or I'll choke you like a hen!"

Soo looked at the men and then at her husband, and then back at the men. One was still talking and fingering cans; the other listened. Sam Fong felt uneasy; he expected them to come over and ask him who was the keenest chap in the store. For this question, and for a long time, Sam Fong had the carefully rehearsed answer: "Me." But saying it was something else. It nerved him up.

On the other hand, the men—one white, one not white—looked odd to Fong: while one was as white as the Englishman with the bad news, he was dressed quite differently. Both of the men in the store were dressed the same, with straw hats and flowered shirts, sunglasses and large watches; they did not wear trousers but rather something Sam Fong recalled as looking like foreshortened Chinese pajamas, striped in bright colors. They wore high socks and had the largest pairs of shoes and, by implication, feet, Fong had ever seen. Fong had seen men dressed just like this on the golf course near the bypass road, striding along followed by a pack of little African boys towing gleaming wheeled carts; the word "golf" was not in Fong's vocabulary, the activity was unknown to him (he imagined the men walking in front of the wheeled carts to be hunters). The two men in the store bore a definite resemblance to those others, in the same clothes, on the grassy meadow. What was especially strange about the men near the shelf was their short hair; their heads seemed shaven (several times they had doffed their hats to wipe their foreheads) and they were both round-shouldered. They were the healthiest men Fong had ever laid eyes on. He had a feeling of what was coming. The white one would come up to him, smile and introduce the non-white one. Then the non-white one would say, "This is my store now" and the white one would wink. Next day the non-white one would come in drunk and fat, bully Fong, tell him this was not his country (it happened—these words—three or four times a week as it was) and that Fong should start sweeping the floor. He shouted again at his wife. He could shout without opening his mouth, like a ventriloquist.

"Find out what they want and send them on their way! They are mixing up all my nice cans with their damned drop-drop!"

Soo approached the men. The men reduced their talk to a whisper and leaned against each other. The non-white one started looking around and smiling, but kept his ear close to the white one's mouth.

Even if Sam Fong and Soo had understood English well, which they didn't, it is doubtful that either of them would have been able to grasp the full meaning of the heavily breathed monologue that was taking place near the Spam. It went something like this:

"You take your average run-of-the-mill Chink and what do you do with him? You stick him in the middle of your biggest continent and you say, 'Smile, be nice, and don't forget there are seven hunert million jest like you that'd give their eyeteeth to be in your place.' Then you leave him there for fifteen, sixteen, give or take a few years, and what happens? I'll tell you what happens. Sure, he doesn't know beans about upward mobility, but he scores. How does he score? I'll tell you how he scores. Because he gets a lot of plain outright cooperation from your average national, African, say. Why? You got *me*. That's one for the books. If I knew the answer to that I wouldn't be in this racket . . ."

The man who was speaking looked over at Soo and stopped talking; then he smiled and turned to Sam Fong who smiled back, and, almost against his will, bowed slightly in the direction of the two healthy men. Sam Fong's right hand was still, as it would be the next ten minutes, unknown to himself and unseen—because of the beautifully large counter, and probably because he had been a long time in Africa—wisely on his fear-frozen groin.

Fifteen minutes after Soo had approached the men and the men had begun talking in a hoarse whisper, one broke away from the shelf of Spam, walked directly—almost quickly—up to Sam Fong, whipped off his straw hat, twisted his whole face sideways, raised his hand up out of his pocket and poked it, open and obvious, over the counter into Fong's gut, and said, nodding his shaven head once, "*Hi!*"

# 4

FAKHRU WAS HAVING A BAD DAY. HE HAD FAILED MISERABLY in an attempt to persuade a Goan shopkeeper to buy a shipment of canned milk. The milk had been canned in Switzerland under the auspices of the Milk for Moroccan Mothers Crusade; machinery, tins, paper for labels and the milk itself had been donated by several large firms in France, Italy, Austria and Germany. A famous French artist had designed a label free of charge and lent his name to the crusade. Diverted from Rabat by some Congolese, the shipment of milk was stored in a Kinshasa warehouse for a year; Fakhru did not hear about the milk until it had reached Katanga, but by then Fakhru was on bowing terms with the UNICEF representative in East Africa who graciously provided trucks to ship the milk overland. Fakhru told him that the milk was intended for the Fakhru Famine Fund. He would distribute it. The trucks arrived in front of Fakhru's door late one night; Fakhru gave each driver one hundred shillings and some worthless Belgian Congo francs for the "mission of mercy," the milk was unloaded, new labels were gummed on by his wife and children bearing the name Fakhru Enterprises Ltd., and the crates were put up for sale. But there were no buyers.

The Goan shopkeeper said the price was too high. Fakhru said it was real milk from England. The Goan said that he did not care if it was horse piss from Lisbon; the price was too high. Fakhru said the cans were strong and would last forever and ever. The Goan said, "Good, then you can sell them in ten years' time, isn't it?"

Fakhru started to leave the store. He paused and turned to the Goan and said in Hindi, "Any day now that big milk train from Nairobi might be derailed off its tracks. In this happenstance, faithful friend Lobo, these white ladies would pay anything for milk. You know they have no breasts—you see them, don't you? They would pay you shillings thirty a can and you would become very rich. For this you would thank your friend Fakhru."

Lobo stood firm. He did not want the milk. Besides, the milk train had only been derailed once and that was in 1943 by some idle Boers in the Highlands who hated the British and thought Hitler was nice. They had since packed their wagons and moved to South Africa.

Fakhru got similar answers from six other shopkeepers including—and this was heartbreaking—an Ismaili who claimed that the time for milk-buying was not ripe; it was an inauspicious time for a big deal. At noon Fakhru was so angry that he went to the nearest slum and tried to get some out-of-work Africans to derail the train. He saw this as a way of getting even with everyone, especially if the Africans were arrested for it.

"No one gets arrested," Fakhru explained to a languid African lighting a thick tube of Indian hemp. "Just a little spill milk, nothing to cry about. What do you say?"

"How we go do dis?" queried another African, accepting a pinch of hemp from Fakhru.

Fakhru shrugged. "Easy. Few rocks on the rails, couple log, and *ptooie* the train go down and all the milk she get spill, isn't it?"

The Africans (there were five of them) were not interested. It sounded big and dangerous. Someone might find out. One was not feeling well; he said he had a fever. Another said he had a sore finger. One of the hempsmokers came straight out and said he thought Fakhru's price was too low.

"That's my price," said Fakhru.

"She too small," said the hempsmoker.

"Thank you *please*," said Fakhru sarcastically, baring his betel-stained fangs. "You want to get rich quick-quick and you don't want to do anything. I ask you to kick Patel. It very difficult to kick Patel because him fat. You kick Patel. I give you shillings fifty. I say punch up Ali the Toothmaker when he call my mother bad names. Ali have big knife from Mombasa. You punch him up. I give you shillings fifty. Now," Fakhru sighed, "I ask you to derail little small train from Nairobi. It too easy—my wife Shoogra would do it if she didn't have so many kids to take care of. Now I ask you this easy thing and you sit there smoking my *bhangi* and tell me to bugger off. You wonder why this country don't develop like U.K., eh? I tell you why—because you're all bloody lazy!"

With that he stormed away. He moved fiercely among the decrepit houses in his white pajamas like an angry prophet. He had told the truth; he was honest and he had bathed with sweet soap and smelled clean. The smell of the decaying slum, the postures of the squatting people cooking over charcoal in doorways angered him. Nearly everyone had let him down. The only ones who had not let him down were the UNICEF people, but even at that he had had to bribe their drivers.

Still in anger Fakhru went to an eating house, and while his brain squirmed in his head trying to conceive a profit amid the clutter of a whole shipment of unsold tinned milk, took his wrath out on the enamel plates of lumpy food. He snatched and spooned lentils, boiled cabbage, chillies and sticky globs of rice into one large bowl and covered this with a dumping of yogurt; this he squeezed quickly and stirred with the tips of his fingers. And then he ate it. He kept his mouth open during the whole meal; he bent over the bowl and threw the squeezed mixture down his throat with a squelching, scooping motion of his fingers. He refused to look up. It was almost as if he were fanning the food into his mouth, so quickly did his fingers move through the mixture; and he did not stop to lick his fingers until he had eaten the last squashed and sodden grain of rice. When he was finished he threw his head back and belched one prolonged roar which began somewhere in the bulge of his pajamas and ended high above his head at the brownish photograph of Gandhi supping with the King. He scraped his chair back, rose noisily, threw four shillings at a Dravidian hunched against the wall and then bought some *pan*—betel nuts and pungent seeds wrapped in a betel leaf— threw that into his mouth and chomped down once. Almost immediately he had a gob of betel juice ready for the nearest wall, and as the glugging in his stomach started, a plan began to take shape in his head.

The yellow one, thought Fakhru, and then laughed. Sam Fong amused him. Fakhru's rage disappeared as his belly rumbled and he staggered toward the grocery store. Fong was not capable of cheating anyone but himself. He worked hard, stayed open at night keeping the store candle-lit when he thought that the number of customers might not justify the burned inch of wick in the hurricane lamp; he did not drink, smoke or go screaming around the brothels with his pants down. What fascinated Fakhru was that in spite of the fact that Fong was compelled to buy everything from him, Fong still managed to swell his bank balance which he never touched— not even at the end of the month when he handed Soo the bags bulging with large green grasshoppers. ("I thought only Africans ate those bugs," Fakhru had said to him.) Fakhru knew the banking habits of everyone he did business with: he had a relative in every bank in town whom he got information out of as easily as he got gobs of red juice out of the dry betel nut. Fakhru knew Fong to be an unshrewd, incautious business-man, gullible and not very bright, but one that still made a profit by a means which Fakhru had never before considered, and, when he knew the means, deemed inhuman. By starving himself, keeping his children naked and all feet in the family unshod; by not using things like soap, combs, hair oil, mirrors and so forth; by not smoking, by gluing crumbs together with fat to make cakes, by throwing away nothing (least of all empty tins which became cups, orange crates which became chairs and insects which became rare food by Fong's performing no more complicated an operation than uttering the words: "This is a cup," "This is a chair," "This is a delicacy"), Sam Fong managed a profit. He swindled only himself and his unsuspecting family. It also allowed him to be foolish and incautious about what he bought. Fakhru knew Sam Fong would buy every single can of milk.

# 5

"Name's Newt, Bert G. Newt, Jr.," said the man to Fong, replacing his straw hat. "This here's Mel Francey."

"Hah!" said the man called Mel Francey in greeting, showing Fong his fine set of teeth. "Ah'm an Amirican Negro and I wanna tell you, friend, the Amiricans's really cleanin up their own backyard. Why, back in the States the white min pick up the trash. Ain't that right, Bert?"

"Sure is Mel, sure as yer standing there. Jest wanted to tell the gemmun what's we're doing in the field of civil rights . . ."

"Civil rights!" said Mel Francey, slapping his thigh. "Why we got Jiminy on the moon and freedom at home. We got every damn thing, scuse me ma'am, we desire, really and truly."

"Creepers, Mel," said Bert Newt. "Ain't nothing really . . ."

"Creepers, nothin!" said Mel Francey. "My ole Granny's seveny-eight next week and she got her own special wheel-chair with an engine, nice little house, people runnin about gitten her every damn thing. Call that nothing?"

"Well..." Bert Newt wagged his head.

"Kids go to the best schools, ride the best buses, get free dental care, the whole shebang. Call that nothin?" Mel Francey shook his jowls and said, "*Heh!* You show me another country where Negroes are better off than they are Stateside..."

"Another country?"

"Ain't none," said Mel Francey emphatically. "Ain't no other country that'd happen in. You go ahead, smart guy, and tell me one—just one is all." He took Bert Newt roughly by the front of his flowered shirt and shook him. He said, "Hell man, you go on tell me! *Tell me!*" Mel Francey was now worked up; his anger was genuine; beads of perspiration clung to the hairs on his arms. He glowered at Bert Newt.

"Well," said Bert Newt, "they say lotsa countries Negroes got better rights..."

"Rights, hell!" shouted Mel Francey, now dropping Newt and stamping on the floor. "I got more damn rights than I can shake a stick at!"

"What ain't you got, man?" asked Bert Newt.

"I ain't got nothin!" This was shouted.

Both Bert Newt and Mel Francey burst into laughter, slapped each other on the back, shook hands and continued with their very loud *haw-haw-haw.* They seemed oblivious of Sam Fong and Soo.

Sam Fong dropped the meat cleaver he had picked up when the man said "Hi," and now he stood gripping the counter watching the two men (Were they madmen? If so, why were they dressed so well?) wiping their eyes, still laughing.

Little wonder that Sam Fong was frightened: his encounters with white men had been anything but cordial. Whites were sinister bastards and they talked too much. Fong understood neither their language nor their disgusting habits. As for their desire, their yearnings—who could understand? Beating Africans, locking them in iceboxes one year; hugging them and popping their eyes out at them the next. One year caning them, the next year patting them on the back and saying, "You deserve it, son." One year picking their pockets, the next year putting it all back, and more. Fong had actually seen a red-faced white man stuff about thirty shillings in the pocket of a black policeman for which the white man was returned a snappy salute. The Emperor would not have stood for it. These were things that Fong had witnessed over a period of thirty-five years in Africa. There were times when these whites had screwed up their courage, come straight up to Sam Fong and asked where opium could be obtained. At first Fong had not understood, but once the loud snuffling was translated into Chinese by the man in the camera store who had overheard the request and knew English, Fong was astonished by the depravity it signaled. In China they had taught him the catechism, baptized him, told him to be a good Catholic and fear God. They had even started teaching him English, nearly all of which—with the exception of the few verbs in the present continuous tense—he forgot; on the other hand, the request of opium was made so frequently that it became one of the few English sentences that Fong knew. But what kind of person would want opium? Only a very rotten idle son of a whore; and this, Fong decided long ago, was what every white man was. It was not until the African in the workshop was sent to England that Fong made his firm resolution; the resolution was formulated not so much from this single instance of white cruelty, the demotion, the loss of his job, as from the resulting wisdom of this long accumulation of disgraceful episodes with whites.

It is one thing to make a resolution; it is quite another to throw money away. Fong was not irrational about making a profit—he did not connive; he did not make a practice of rubbing his hands and bowing; he did not stand on the sidewalk and drag people into his store. But he knew that if he did not make a small profit he would, quite simply, die like a dog. He decided that when the two men stopped their talking and he ventured into Swahili he might come out a few shillings the better for his patience. What he did not understand was, why all the talk? Why this noisy kowtow and dumbshow? What were they shouting about and in what language? Fong was consoled by the fact that they were arguing with each other, perhaps arguing over the ownership of the store. It was certainly true that the non-white one bore more than a passing resemblance to the keen chap in the workshop who had come back drunk and disorderly and well dressed from England to snatch his job away. The argument had alternated between war and song; Fong could not tell if they loved or hated each other, though he finally decided on the latter. There was no denying that these men were enemies, but it was also true that they did not seem to have weapons, and, as the proverb has it, yuan from a coolie are as welcome as yuan from a prince. That was why Sam Fong dropped the meat cleaver.

Soo had not stirred. From time to time she had winced. Once she saw the men had no intention of speaking to her she crept back behind the counter, stayed there silent and yellow and continued to peer at the two loud men.

She saw the two men turn away from each other and start talking to her husband. She was afraid, although she was not sure who would get the worst of it.

"We're not here to sell you America," said Bert Newt.

"No sir!" said Mel Francey.

"You buying nice bread?" Fong asked. This was almost the limit of his English. He added in Swahili, "Good, good bread, baking yesterday."

His words went unheard.

"Fact is," said Bert Newt, "we're not here to sell you a thing!"

"Not a damn thing," said Mel Francey.

"You buy good tea, better price anywhere in Africa," said Fong, exhausting his English.

"All we want to do is get acquainted, get on a hand-shaking, how-are-you, face-to-face relationship, a first-name basis, you know what I mean? I want you to call me Bert. This here's Mel . . ."

The two hands were again extended. Fong did not see them. The hands were withdrawn.

"Point is, we want to leave all our differences aside. Oh, I know what you're saying to yourself. You're saying: Who those two Yankee big-mouths think they are, banging into my store and shooting their mouths off! Their country is damn rich and big! You're thinking we're just two gungho guys..."

Recognition flickered across Fong's face for a moment at the utterance. He said nothing.

"...I know you're thinking of the Iron Curtain and the Cold War. Well, let me tell you, just between you and me: that's for the big fellers in Washington and Peking. You and me, we're the little fellers..."

"Yeah!" boomed Mel Francey. "That's raht!"

"...We got no grief with you just cause your eyes are different and your skin's yaller..."

"Color of a man's skin don't mean a damn thing!"

"...We come here into your humble little store," said Bert Newt, apparently winding up, "to extend the hand of friendship across the ocean and across the sea. We want *you* to come to *our* little houses and homes to have a modest but nourishing meal someday. And let me repeat, we don't come as Americans, we do not come to sell America... Jeepers creepers, try to *forget* that we're Americans! Just call me Bert and I'll be happy as a clam... I'll tell my wife..."

Sam Fong saw that the talk was about to end; the voices were getting softer, though the words no more intelligible. He leaned toward the men and very quickly, in Swahili, English and Chinese, repeated a list of the items that could be had: "Bread, butter, egg, hair straightener, buns, juice, bread, potato, rice, razor blade, sweet, rice, recapped tire, soap, egg, bread, smoking, nice tea..."

Bert Newt and Mel Francey smiled.

"See you around," said Bert Newt.

"*Sayonara*," said Mel Francey, clapping his hands together in front of his face and bowing, as had once seen Marlon Brando do.

They began backing out of the store.

Sam Fong looked dejectedly at them; they were smiling at him and still backing out. Fong did not hear Bert Newt say to Mel in a whisper, "Now you see what the State Department is up against. These guys won't budge an inch. You go on and tell me our work isn't cut out for us . . ." And Mel answered, "I know just what you mean, brother. . ." They were still backing up and smiling. Mel Francey still had his hands together in front of his face.

Outside the window Fakhru swung down the sidewalk. Sam Fong experienced an odd sensation on seeing someone he had always thought to be his enemy. He waited for hatred but felt only joy when he saw Fakhru. *He can save me, he will know what to do.* It was the feeling of relief that the farmer in his filthy hut, beset by mysterious strangers, has for the fat landlord rolling up in a great golden carriage

Fakhru turned to splash a gob of betel juice into the gutter, but he was still walking briskly and when he turned to wipe his mouth on the back of his sleeve he crashed into Bert Newt and Mel Francey.

"Sorry, *bwana*." Fakhru was the first to speak. He spoke to Bert Newt.

"Name's Newt. Bert G. Newt, Jr. This here's Mel Francey. . ."

"*Hah!*" said Mel. "I'm a Negro from Alabama where they say we got a lot of trouble, only we don't, that's all. Your average newspaper's a damn liar!"

Fakhru extended his hand: "Hassanali Fakhru of Fakhru Enterprises Limited."

"Chalk one up," Bert said under his breath. They shook hands.

"Welcome to this humble grocery," said Fakhru. "I hope from the bottom of my heart that you have been treated as a brother."

"This your store?" asked Bert.

"In a manner of speaking, yes, please. But I am compelled to add that it is currently leased to my old friend and colleague, Sam Fong, the yellow one there at the back."

"Frenayers?" asked Mel Francey.

"Beg pardon?"

"He said, *is this man a friend of yours?*" Bert was eager.

"Most definitely he is, although as you can see he is quite obviously a *kaffir*. But this is no matter—we are here to build a multiracial society with *harambee* and Africans and goodness knows what . . ."

"I'll shake on that," said Mel Francey, pumping Fakhru's hand.

Sam Fong watched closely. Fakhru knew how to handle these people; there was no question of that, Fong felt safe with Fakhru in the store. He saw the three men move toward him.

"What do they want?" asked Fong in Swahili when the three stood before him.

"You understand this language of Swahili, of course," Fakhru said laughing.

"Hell no!" said Mel.

"I know *jambo*," said Bert.

"Well, that's a good beginning," said Fakhru, and then in Swahili he said to Fong, "*Me* know what they want? How am *I* to know what they want? This is your store, not mine!"

"I listened with both ears but understood nothing of what they said."

"Did they buy anything?"

"No."

"Did they sell you anything?"

"No."

"Did they give you anything?"

"No. Ask them where they're from."

Fakhru asked.

The Americans brightened and both started talking at once, interrupting each other and gesturing.

"They say they're from America."

"Why don't they speak English?"

"They do, but it's different English. Anyway, friend Fong, what makes you a *fundi* on English?" Fakhru giggled, then turned to his new friends. "Is there anything at all you would like to communicate with my old friend Sam Fong?"

"Tell him we want to be frins, that we come in peace and don't mean no harm," said Mel.

"Beg pardon?"

"He said, tell the man we want to be his friend. . . . *We just want to talk to him!*" Bert spoke loudly, thinking that if he spoke loudly he would be better understood.

Fakhru turned back to Sam Fong. "They say they would like to talk to you at greater length with a view toward selling you, at extremely low prices, goods from American bleck market."

Sam Fong smiled. It was the first emotion he had shown since the Americans entered the store. Bert Newt and Mel Francey saw him smile. Both reached over the counter, dragged his hand out from behind and shook it vigorously.

"He says he's ready to talk anytime. He wants to be your friend."

# 6

THE AMERICANS WENT AWAY AT PEACE WITH THEMSELVES and making plans.

"You're very lucky," Fakhru said to Sam Fong, still in Swahili. "These people want to sell you good merchandise, *American* merchandise from American bleck market. That is very bleck market indeed. Americans have even been known to lend money at low interest if they like someone . . ."

"I do not need money," said Fong. "But a little black market merchandise is always welcome, no?"

"Interesting that you should bring up that subject. It happens that I have just received a shipment of *number one* canned milk all the way from the *world famous* UNICEF dairies in England, United Kingdom . . ."

It took just ten minutes to convince Sam Fong that he should buy all the cans. They were black market cans which was assurance of their high quality; and who could tell, Fakhru's argument ran, the milk train from Nairobi might be derailed any day, that is, knocked off its rails by unfortunate happenstance. The white women who had no breasts, as any fool could see, and therefore were incapable of suckling their children, would pay anything for this canned milk. When it came to children, Fakhru said, white people acted very strangely indeed.

Once again Sam Fong felt a kinship with Fakhru. When they were doing business and Fong knew he was being swindled he had nothing but bald hatred for the Ismaili. Yet as soon as white men were mentioned, as soon as they entered a business transaction, Fong felt that it was he and Fakhru against them all: whites were the real enemy. And, since Independence, by an odd quick process which Fakhru said in English was known as getting "jumped-up," the Africans had taken their place as second enemy, and Fong felt the same uneasy awe for their sudden power ("I can have you deported tomorrow, you bloody bugger") and boundless contempt for what he felt to be their true instinctive existence: a daily filthy slumber in the shade of the nearest tree, then a paid roll in the mud with their reeking women, their lives dominated by bananas which could be had by stretching out their long arms. It was a lifetime of spear-throwing and sleeping and sweaty small moments humping their women like hares until a white man came by, gave them new clothes to cover up the dirt, gave them police protection and power and jobs they did not deserve. The white man's most evil deed was clothing the African. The clothed African was dangerous: he had pockets, and these pockets the white man stuffed with twenty-shilling notes. No clothes, no corruption, Fong had reasoned: how do you go about bribing a naked man? But now the African and the white were good friends, they loved each other and the white man made a lot of money in this. The African was happy in his dirt, eating dung and throwing his spears—why should he complain? He had lost nothing. Sam Fong and Fakhru were left, the only visible immigrants, surrounded by enemies, and Fong felt very close to Fakhru.

So close, in fact, did Fong feel that when he gave Fakhru the check for the milk he knew he was swindling him. The milk cost 1000 shillings; the check was made out to Fakhru

Enterprises Ltd. for 1000 shillings; Fong knew perfectly well that he had 632 shillings ninepence only in the bank and that the check would bounce. But by the end of the month, when the long rains started, the train from Nairobi would be derailed, and, by then, Sam Fong would have much more than the difference in his account. In a way, it was the first time that Sam Fong had given a serious thought—by planning ahead—to making a profit. He was sure it would pay off. In the meantime he could use 632 shillings ninepence in his account as an emergency fund, as he always considered it.

There had been only one emergency in his life: buying the merchandise, leasing the store and becoming a *dukawallah*. Since those first anxious days there had been no threat to his calm. The bank balance assured him of continued calm. Shortly after he arrived in East Africa he saw Africans as enemies and realized that he had seven million of them. As calm as he felt he was still realistic in believing that it could not last and that he would most likely be deported. And Fakhru was in the same boat: calm because he was prepared for the inevitable disaster.

Feeling almost brotherly toward Fakhru, Fong handed over the check that he knew would bounce. He did it with the grim smile of the entrepreneur. It was the only way he could get the milk.

"You will not regret this," said Fakhru in Swahili. And in Hindi: "Blessings on your house; may it be kept safe from Africans . . ."

"When will the goods be delivered?" asked Fong.

"Straightaway," said Fakhru. "Which is to say, now-now." He left.

Sam Fong looked across the counter to Soo and said, "I am happy."

# 7

Fakhru was not surprised when the bank teller informed him that the check could not be cashed as there were insufficient funds in the account. He did feel let down, for he had decided—absurd thought—that the Chinaman was honest, that he swindled only himself. Fakhru also thought of himself as a good judge of character and prided himself on knowing "the native mind."

It was not the first time someone had pulled this shoddy *dukawallah* ruse. How many others had there been? Hundreds, thousands, and not one of them with sufficient imagination to try a really extravagant swindle. This petty cheating depressed Fakhru; he knew full well he would prevail over the felony, but this was no test of business prowess. What Fakhru prayed for was a gigantic swindle for which he could summon all his powers, and which, by a counterswindle, would make him the wealthiest man in East Africa (donations to His Highness's favorite charity; painless bribing; a coffee estate, an American car). Fong's was an ordinary slimy trick, ludicrously small, and, worse, Fong wrote so big that it was impossible to alter the check.

"You can't give him overdraft?"

"No," said the teller.

"He's not bleck, you know. No worry about a little overdraft."

"Sorry," said the teller.

"He's almost white—yellow to be exact. How about an overdraft? Little bit, not so much."

The teller was silent.

"Yes, but certainly there must be some mistake. Bye-bye," said Fakhru bowing, withdrawing and pulling his empty leather briefcase off the counter. He hurried back to his cluttered office to think.

Rubbing the picture of H.H. the Aga Khan for luck, he dialed his cousin Goolshan at the bank.

"Goolshan, my flesh and blood, son of my mother's noble brother now dead, alas, and unable to see what a success his son has been—didn't I see you on the evening of the great and auspicious Gurpurb Celebrations at a tiny but very comfortable bar outside town with, if you will pardon an unsolicited compliment, an exceedingly charming African girl in a rather tight dress? Or did my eyes deceive me? Allow me to praise your discretion, not to mention your . . . what's that?"

The voice at the other end of the line barked something hoarsely in Hindi.

Fakhru laughed, winked at His Highness and said, "The yellow one whose father's name is Fong . . ."

After a few moments Fakhru said, "Yes," listened, then, with elaborate thanks and an apology for having mistaken some profligate for his upright cousin Goolshan, rang off. He looked at Fong's frayed check, spat, did a little figuring on the back of an envelope he rescued from the wastebasket, took his own checkbook, called his houseboy (an elderly man in shorts) and set off for the post office.

Fakhru did not like to wait in line. As soon as he arrived in the post office he directed his houseboy to the correct line, pressed threepence into the old man's hand and went over to lean against the wall. Mehboob was there; so were the three Patels, Visrani, Mehta the barber, Mistry the carpenter; and, off to the side, Ali, the half-caste butcher, whose shop was not far from Sam Fong's. They traded agonies. Visrani adjusted his dhoti and said that business was very slack; the rest concurred: business was in a terrible slump. "We'll be eating shit very soon," offered Mistry. From this they went on to the rupee which they discussed for a full ten minutes. Tenderness entered their voices; it was as if they were talking about an old friend. One of the Patels said it might be devalued. "The poor rupee; it's the fault of those people in India—they don't know what life is about," Mehta said. "No one here knows either," another Patel said. "The world is out of tune," said Visrani, chewing. Mistry said that there was a strike in the workshop across the street, "and the winds are starting to blow in the direction of my own workshop."

Fakhru agreed with everyone, excused himself and went to look for a litter basket. He found one attached to the wall near a long table; it was half-filled with crumpled, scratched-out cable forms. He took aim and spat. Then he unfolded his checkbook from his pajamas and wrote a check for 368 shillings and made it out to Sam Fong. He looked for his house boy; the houseboy was still far from the window.

When he returned to the group he asked them what they were doing. They said they were either buying stamps or registering letters or posting parcels; that is, their African assistants were doing these things. In the line closest to the wall were the nine khaki-clad barefoot Africans holding envelopes and papers and talking. They were enjoying themselves immensely; the lines were all very long, and it was cool in the post office. The majority of those waiting before the windows were Africans wearing khaki office uniforms; there were also a few potbellied American women with cork helmets, suede boots and clean bush jackets on which were sewn rows of cloth loops for shotgun shells but no shotgun shells. Some Germans with overlarge knapsacks and beards stood in a group and shouted loudly at each other; they clutched postcards. A small lady pushed a stack of Christmas cards under one clerk's wire mesh; she said she was sending them by surface mail to the Hebrides. From time to time the Asians lining the walls glanced at their deputies in the stamp queues.

"The little blecks," said Fakhru using the Hindi diminutive, "they love to stand in line."

"It's their line, it's their country," said Mehta with gloom in his voice.

"If we really wanted to," said S. R. Patel, "we could take over this whole filthy place."

"Who wants it," said Mehta lugubriously.

"I'll tell you a sad story," said J. H. Patel. "You know I'm running a wholesale place—just like yours, brother [he nodded toward Fakhru]. I sell the usual: razor blades, Madrassi towels, nice fabrics, good quality American-type soap, a little bit of coffee and the rest. So this African woman [he said this in English, pronouncing it *Effrriken vhooman*] is buying lots of goods from me. I put this down in my book. Then she buys rice in large bags and some bread, *daily* you understand. I put this in my accounts and I deliver it all in my pickup. The last trip I make—this has been going on for about three weeks—I give her the bill. She says she has no money, but her brother maybe I should see him. She gives me his name, address in the Parliament Office Building, in the Ministry of External Affairs. Why is this brother of hers in the Ministry of External Affairs? There is a very good reason for this: he is the big minister. Off I go to see him. His secretary, a fat and very pleasant muhindi tells me to wait. I wait. Then she tells me to go in. I go in. When I enter I see the minister brother sitting at a big desk. He tells me to take a seat, then he says to me, 'What's your problem, my good man?' Very British, these blacks . . ."

Mistry laughed, the rest nodded and took this pause as an opportunity to spit.

". . . I say to him, 'Let's call this our problem, not my problem.' He says, 'Es you vish.' I say, 'Your sister owes me about fifteen hundred shillings only.' He says, 'So what?' I say, 'So I want my fifteen hundred, if you don't mind, good sir; my family likes to eat now and then.' He says, 'You *wahindi* are all rich and you give us hell of trouble—what's fifteen hundred to you? My sister'—he continues—'she's just new at this sort of thing; give the poor girl a chance. Don't you know we Africans believe in African socialism? We always pay. Everyone is brothers; *she* your brother; she'll pay you.' I say, 'If you don't mind I am taking the liberty to correct you: *she said you pay me*. She said I must see you.' 'She gave you my name?' asks this big black. I say, 'Yes, indeed.' 'Did she say I was going to pay you?' 'Not exactly,' I say; 'she just gave me your name, she wanted me to see you.' 'Take a look,' says the black; then he says, 'Now you see me—are you satisfied? Give my sister whatever she wants; we Africans are poor; this is a poor country, a *developing* country, dirty and poor, and you are wasting my time. Our colonial masters just stole like hell from us, but now most of them see the error and sinning they did on us.' He keeps talking: 'These white men wouldn't come in here and say what you're saying—they know better than that. They know all kinds of problems we have, even some we don't know and myself, some I don't know, and I'm a minister. Now take my advice,' he says, 'I'm a busy man, my sister she's also a busy woman and we can't be bothered with your financial problems; as for me, I was born in a mud hut with no clothes and had to shit in the grass, so don't try to tell me your family is hungry...' Then this black says that he has to meet the Prime Minister, so I better go home and stop troubling. I go home and what do I find? I find the sister in my shop. She needs more fabrics..."

"That *is* a sad story," said Fakhru. And he thought, Yes, that is a sad story indeed.

Mehta said that the same thing happened to his cousin in the Congo. A big *bwana* on the government said his cousin had to supply fresh meat everyday or they would kick him. "Only pretty soon," Mehta continued, "there was no government, at least no *bwanas* giving orders up and down; no big *bwanas*, no problems, business she keeps going on. That's how it was in the Congo," he said.

"What are you going to do?" Visrani asked J. H. Patel, ignoring Mehta's footnote.

"What is he going to do! What do you think he is going to do?" Mistry shouted, grinning for no reason at all. "He's going to give this black sister what she wants! No, J. H.?"

"What else can I do?" said J. H. Patel. "I'm a poor man."

All smiled and stroked their chins.

"These Africans," said Fakhru, "they want everything free, if you ask me. They have no business sense. They are killing us."

"They don't know what business is," said S. R. Patel.

"No, man," said Ali the half-caste, in his one offering to the group.

"And we get blamed for everything," said Fakhru.

"Just bloody swindlers, that's all," said Visrani. "These blacks. They should be kicked *kabisa*."

Fakhru looked over and saw that his houseboy had gotten the stamps. He excused himself, offered his condolences to J. H. Patel and went to the opposite side of the post office. He watched a well-dressed African opening his letters. The African tore them open and sighed, threw the envelopes into the wastebasket and lumbered heavily out. Fakhru went to the wastebasket and poked around with his finger. He turned up two nice envelopes; on each one the address was written in very small letters, and neither of them had its flap gummed. Fakhru put a filled-out deposit slip inside with the check for 368 shillings, crossed out the address, added the address of the bank and affixed the stamps which had been bought (and moistened) by the houseboy. He dropped the envelope into the box marked *Local Letters* and looked at his watch: it was nine thirty.

Fifteen minutes passed. An African with a big canvas sack came over and opened a small door at the bottom of the letter box. Gathering up the letters in his two hands the African stuffed them into the sack and then threw the sack over his shoulder and lugged it into the sorting room. Fakhru went outside and found the bank's post office box. It was number 250. While he watched it a half hour passed; beggars had gathered and were bleating around his knees. For luck Fakhru dropped threepence into a leper's cup, and at that moment an African wearing a gray uniform and a red fez shuffled up to the box. Fakhru pulled out his own key and pretended to be opening the box just above that of the bank. He glanced down and saw his letter, crossed out address and all, in the bank messenger's hand. The messenger removed his fez, then slowly knelt and peered into the box; when he was satisfied that it was empty he creaked the rusted door of the box very slowly shut, played with the key for a while and then shuffled back to the bank. His bare feet scraping on the gritty cement pavement made such an unpleasant sound that Fakhru decided not to follow too closely.

At typewriters and adding machines in the large walled-in area of the bank, thirty Asian girls pecked at keys, flipped through thick files and sipped at cups of tea. Fakhru watched the fezzed messenger distributing the envelopes among the girls. He looked at his watch again: it was quarter to eleven.

Fakhru knew that the check had to be cleared through his own account; he had purposely written a check on the account he had in that bank so that the process would be simplified. He allowed fifteen minutes for this. The check would then have to be passed to whoever handled Sam Fong's account, another ten minutes, and finally it would have to be added in and computed on the balance sheet, another fifteen minutes. By eleven thirty Sam Fong would have a thousand shillings in his account; by eleven thirty-five Sam Fong would be penniless.

All the calculations were correct. Fakhru went to the teller at eleven thirty and presented Fong's check. The teller scribbled on it and passed it to another red-fezzed African; when the check was dropped before the teller again there were more initials on it.

"How do you want it?" asked the teller.

"Five hundred, three hundred in twenties, one hundred in tens and the rest in fives," said Fakhru opening his old leather briefcase.

# 8

"THESE CHINAMEN ONLY UNDERSTAND ONE LANGUAGE," SAID Bert.

"Killin, burnin and violence," said Mel with conviction.

"No," said Bert, "Chinese. You know, we didn't say a straight word to him the whole time."

"Easy does it," said Mel. "This here's gonna amaze the shit out of the old man."

"You're telling me."

"A real honest-to-God Chinese. First one I set eyes on this side of the Chu-Chin-Chow in Mobile." Mel shook his head. "But you know what? They look the same wherever you go and that's a truth."

"How about that smile?"

"How about that! Did you *see* him? We had him in the palm of our hand. Him and . . . and . . . What was the other one's name?"

"Dunno. Got it here somewhere." Bert Newt lifted his flowered shirt. Underneath, attached to his plaid belt, was a small tape recorder. A thin wire leading from the tape recorder was adhesive-taped over the bulge of his abdomen; a tiny microphone dangled near his navel. Newt unstrapped the tape recorder and peeled the tape and wire from his skin. He placed the box on the table and allowed his thick fingers to puzzle over it like hairless creatures eager to devour it; they hovered close. With a quick gesture Newt held the box fast with his left hand and squeezed a plastic rectangle with his right. The tape recorder squawked.

Mel Francey put his head close, just in time to hear the loud noise of Fakhru bumping into them, and then:

"*. . . Sorry, bwana . . . Name's Newt. Bert G. Newt, Jr. This here's Mel Francey . . . Hah! I'm a Negro from Alabama where they say we got a lot of trouble, only we don't, that's all. Your average . . .*"

"What about the hands?" Mel reached for the tape recorder.

"Wait a sec," said Bert, snatching it away and winding it forward.

"*. . . Hassanali Fakhru of Fakhru Enterprises Limited. . . . Chalk up one . . .*"

There was a little slap on the tape, the handshake, barely audible.

"That's the baby," said Mel.

"Yeah, lemme play it again," Bert mumbled.

He wound the tape back again. Again the handshake was played, this time louder, a little *pip*, like a dung beetle releasing a pellet onto a hard surface. Mel Francey beamed and demanded to hear it several more times.

"*Pip . . . pip . . . pip.*"

Mel said the old man would eat that one up. He sat down and fanned himself with his hat. "How was I?" he asked.

"Beautiful, great."

"You think I was okay? I mean, did I hit him hard enough with the Alabama business?"

"Terrific. I seen a lotta guys come through this office, Mel baby, but believe me, you got everyone of them beat by a mile. You can take that from me, and I been in this racket one hell of a long time."

"Think so?" Mel Francey shook his head. It created an odd effect, because, as he shook his head, he still fanned himself with his straw hat. He looked at Bert Newt and said, "Course, you didn't do so bad yourself, brother."

"How about that *jambo* bit?"

"Nearly cracked me up, that's all. Wow," said Mel, "we got 'em by the ass." He squinted: "Say, Bert? Where *did* you get that *jambo* bit?"

"Book," said Bert fiddling with the tape recorder. "It's *howsaboy* in Kiswahili."

"I liked that a lot."

"Think the old man'll like it?"

"*Think!* I *know* it's gonna amaze the shit outta him!"

"What about a CFFRR on the thing?"

"Sure," said Mel. "I'll get the card."

Mel Francey went to the file cabinet and took out a rectangular card. At the top of the card was printed: CONFIDENTIAL FACE TO FACE RATIO RATING.

"Lessee here," said Mel. He read, "Christian names, other names, address, tele . . . What'd that guy say his name was?"

The tape was played again.

"Now which one you suppose is his Christian name?" Mel inquired:

"The one he said first. That's usually the case."

"Ginrilly," said Mel. He mumbled slowly as he wrote: "Christchun nayum. Has-san-alley . . . Oth-er nayums Fakroo. There we are."

"What've we got next?"

"Verbalization rating."

"Give him about sixty. We got well past *Hi*."

"Six-ty," said Mel, writing. "Motivation?"

"High."

"Response reinforcement?"

"'Bout seventy. He smiled, remember?"

"Yeah. Big shit-eatin grin."

"Let's do the Chinaman," said Bert Newt.

# 9

At roughly the same time as Fakhru was standing in the bank dealing the careful final blows to Sam Fong's checking account, Fong found himself counting out wrinkled five-shilling notes to a man of about forty, barefoot and in rags except for a new red shirt. The man said he was a Young Pioneer; he carried a knobbed stick painted with the colors of a national flag. He said that unless Fong gave him fifty shillings his windows would be broken, and, adding a euphemism in the vernacular, his wife would be "handled."

Sam Fong had stared at the Young Pioneer and said nothing. He went to the back room, took a brick out of the wall and from the opening withdrew all that was there in the cobwebs and mold; a damp fifty shillings. It was all he had.

The Young Pioneer leaned his stick against the counter and took the money with both hands cupped, in the traditional manner and not without grace. He reminded Fong that this was the African way and said, "Thank you, brother." Fong dipped his head in the direction of the Young Pioneer.

"I know you only come here to make money. You send money to white banks overseas and you don't care if we cope up at all." The Young Pioneer leered at Soo. "Then you don't want to marry Africans and I don't know why. You just want to stay with your own people. You don't care about us . . ."

"I just gave you fifty shillings," said Fong.

The Young Pioneer looked at the crumpled bills in his hand and said, "Yes, *bwana*, *you* didn't give us any trouble. We like people that help us, even the bloody Communists if they help us we say thank you. But if you businessmen don't want to help us we don't want you here and I don't care if . . ."

"Thirty-five years in this country," Sam Fong said smiling, gesturing around the shop, at his wife, and nodding toward two of his small children who were playing on the floor and croaking.

The Young Pioneer raised his arm stiffly in a mechanical salute and shouted, "Forward *ayver*, backward *nayver!*" Then he tossed a little card on the counter, picked up his knobbed stick and left. Outside, he climbed into a new minibus. On one of the seats, his bulk and the fact that no one sat with him testifying to his importance, sat a man in a fur hat, leaning on a beaded cane. On the other seats were more men wearing red shirts: they were crammed in, five to a seat. On the side of the bus was written in yellow:

DIES IST EIN GESCHENK DER WESTDEUTSCHEN BEVÖLKERUNG
THIS IS A GIFT OF THE PEOPLE OF WEST GERMANY.

The minibus lurched away.

Soo took the card. She stared at it a full minute and then translated it into Chinese: "Now you are a non-transferable membership card of the People's Congress Party. How much did it cost?"

"Fifty shillings, which means no more money behind the brick."

Soo clucked.

"These Africans have an odd way of collecting taxes," said Fong.

Money had been collected from Fong many times before, and each demand for money was matched by something tragic happening. The first tragedy Fong remembered was in 1960. A fat man, an African, had come to the carpentry shop together with a white man wearing glasses and dressed in shorts. They wanted chairs, they said. But once in the workshop they assembled all the workers and gave speeches. They said that the day was coming when all the people of the country would break off the chains of slavery; everyone would soon be free and the snakes would be driven out. The white man—this surprised Sam Fong—not only spoke in Swahili, but he also said that white men had enslaved the African from the beginning of time; the guilty ones were the whites, said the white man. He went on to say that the whites were thieves and hyenas. The fat African who carried a fly whisk shouted, "Yes, yes! But the dawn is breaking and we will no longer be slaves," and the white man added, "Long live the black power of the People's Congress Party!" At this point the two men collected money from all the workers; Fong had looked dolefully at the ragged workers emptying their pockets into the fur hat of the African. Sam Fong had contributed three shillings sixpence to the cause. The white man and the African went away, the workers went back to their hammering and sawing, and then the tragedy occurred: the country became independent. Taxes were raised, soldiers suddenly popped up everywhere, the workers were frightened and many resigned and went back to their villages where there were no soldiers and no taxes. Sam Fong saw the fat face of the African in the newspaper everyday; the white man's picture also appeared once in a while. Shortly thereafter another white man had inquired, "Who is your keenest chap?" and six months later Sam Fong was out of a job.

The money collecting always seemed to mean that trouble was not far off. A year after Independence there were rumors that two ministers had resigned from the government and were campaigning against the Prime Minister somewhere in the bush, giving speeches in banana groves. Sam Fong did not believe the rumors until the Young Pioneers showed up with their hands out demanding money; the rumors proved correct. It was about this time that Fong—under pressure from his customers—scratched the progress slogans off his storefront. His African customers said they were fed up; there was no freedom.

Except for the money contributed on these two occasions and the loss of his job, Fong did not suffer physical attack; no one "handled" his wife, and independence and freedom seemed simply more expensive than what existed before. "Run for your life! Everyone is being beaten up," the rumors sometimes said, but Sam Fong in four years as a shopkkeeper in this free country had never seen anyone beaten up. As far as he was concerned this was the problem: the British had made a regular practice of beating people. The results had been amazing; the protectorate had prospered. Sam Fong believed privately that there should be public whippings, that incorrigibles should be locked in iceboxes to suffocate now and then. But it did not happen. Nothing happened. The government wanted money or anything else it could get, taxes, presents, free food, bags of rice, goats, songs. No one "handled" Fong's wife, no one kicked in the window of his store, no one laid a finger on him; business was awful.

"So this is freedom," said Sam Fong to Soo. "They take your money and *pftt* you are free. And now there are no shillings behind the brick."

But the feeling of impending disaster persisted: if they are collecting money something is going to happen. When there is a revolution, the people leave town and the streets are deserted; when there is a revolution it is the grocer who suffers most.

The arrival of Fakhru's van the next day put these morose thoughts out of Fong's mind or, rather, converted the gloomy thoughts into hopeful business prospects. This canned milk transaction was Fong's first genuine deal, assuming, as Fong did, that there must be something fundamentally dishonest about every business deal. If there was trouble, Fong now reasoned, the milk train from Nairobi would not get through.

Fong had never seen so many cans. For the first time in

four years Fong felt as if he truly was a grocer, and his mind started using that perverse logic that is characteristic of small grocers: Fong felt as if he were getting the canned milk free. By the time the trouble came, the train derailed, the milk sold and the money deposited there would be ten times as much in the bank as was there originally; he would never miss the small investment—he would have a great pile of shillings instead. Fakhru's driver panted and huffed as he dragged the boxes into the store; he heaped the boxes against one wall. At first Fong was going to help unload the boxes from the van, but when he remembered that the boxes had yet to be sold and that he had no money stuffed behind the brick, he suddenly went limp, unwilling. He stood quietly and watched the boxes being unloaded. He counted twenty-seven of them. Each time the African driver slammed a box down Fong's head moved slightly.

"We can call it Sam Fong Friendly Milk Store," said Soo from the back.

"Don't be a fool," said Sam Fong.

Hearing this Soo came forward. Fong slapped her. She withdrew.

What am I getting excited about? Fong thought. The check bounced, I have money in the bank, Soo can make a sign: SAM FONG FRIENDLY MILK STORE. If money is being collected there is going to be serious trouble. Many people will leave town, but whites will not leave town. Whites will stay; everyone loves them. Their children drink a lot of milk, cow's milk, which is why they sometimes have a bovine look about them. Whites are not frightened by revolutions. They will buy this mountain of canned milk. The money will come, I will deposit it, Fakhru will cash his check. And Fakhru will appreciate my method of operating because has not Fakhru on many occasions swindled me?

He shouted for Soo. Soo entered the shop from the back again and stood bravely before Fong, expecting the finale to the beating.

"Get a board," said Fong

Soo went outside and got a thick board. He never hit me with a board before, thought Soo.

"Not big enough," said Fong when he saw the board.

That man is very upset, thought Soo, heaving the largest board she could find.

"Now your brush," said Fong, satisfied with the board.

A new torture, thought Soo, remembering stories of chopsticks that had been pushed through the ears of the unlawful in her native land.

"Some paint," said Fong.

I am finished, thought Soo, he will kill me with the materials that would have gone to mock him; that's what I get for opening my mouth. But she could find no paint. She found only a half-pint of turpentine. She presented this to her husband and said, "This will have to do. I assure you that it will be an equally painful substitute. When you have beaten me with the board and inserted that pointed brush into my ear and pushed it to the other side it will make no difference if you cover me with paint or turpentine. In any case, I shall die, as I deserve to."

"Are you out of your mind?" Fong said. "I want to make a Sam Fong Friendly Milk Store sign. Now where is the paint?"

Soo looked in the back room and found only mice; Fong looked in the shop. The can of paint was not to be found anywhere. The last sign Soo had made was the Friend Frocery sign; Fong had suppressed— either through mockery or beatings, or both—all Soo's attempts to make any other signs (SAM FONG MATTRESS SHOP; SAM FONG TIRES FOR ALL OCCASIONS) and somewhere in the course of four years the paint had been lost. But Fong did not give up the search. He was still on his hands and knees combing the trash near the baseboard, the large dead roaches and mango peels. So absorbed was he that he did not see two figures enter the store until he came upon their shoes. He scrabbled and flung refuse this way and that and finally he turned his eyes upward. Above him were two Chinamen in white starched shirts and wide trousers.

"Comrade," they said as one.

Fong stood. He was fascinated by them. He did not bother

to brush the dirt off his knees. His head tilted to the side in amused bewilderment. He greeted them as masters and said that it was a blessing that they should enter his shop; it was God's wish.

The small triangular faces of the two men seemed to get smaller. Their mouths fell involuntarily open and showed decaying teeth.

"We were driving by," said the taller of the two, "and I saw your sign. I said to Comrade Chen, 'That is a comrade; we should greet him.'"

"When did you leave China?" asked the second.

"The Year of the Dragon, nineteen thirty," said Sam Fong.

"That was a good year for us—big campaigns in the middle Yangtze in the summer, victory over two reactionary divisions in the winter, many defectors to our side . . ."

"Many people left then, too," added the taller one slowly.

"I left," said Fong.

"Whose side were you on?"

"There were so many sides, I could not make up my mind —I was on no one's side. I was a carpenter in our small village workshop, making excellent cupboards of our rare and wormproof teak. One day my father said to me, 'Son, the Manchus are gone forever and from now on it seems to be every man for himself . . .'"

"You joined Chiang Kai-shek?"

"No, we walked to Foochow, got on a boat and here I am. My father died while on the boat, God rest his soul." At this point Fong made the sign of the cross slowly and mumbled a little prayer. When he emerged moist-eyed from his little beatific reverie he looked at the two men and asked, "Who is the emperor now?"

The Chinamen looked at each other, almost sadly.

"You remember Mao, of course," one began.

"The library assistant fellow? They were offering fifty thousand yuan for his capture the year I left—twenty thousand for only his head! Now there's a *real* troublemaker, my father used to say."

The faces of the two men seemed to become yet smaller. In

a new tone of voice, restrained, though shriller than before, the taller one said, "He is Chairman now and we are bathed in the light of his glorious thought!"

"So they didn't catch him?"

"They couldn't. The peasants were ripe for revolution."

"Well, as I said, my father and I were in Foochow at the time, just leaving." Fong laughed—barked, rather—but he was alone in this.

A customer entered the store. It was Margerine, an old, graying African man wearing broken eyeglasses mended with bits of Scotch tape; he had been given his name by an English *memsahib* who was unable to pronounce his clan name M'gheren'he, and said she thought it sounded terribly like Margerine. He often ran errands for Fong in return for jelly beans or small cubes of greasy homemade soap. Today Margerine had twopence. He wanted a cigarette.

"One cigarette, twopence, and a match for nothing," Fong said cheerfully, lighting the cigarette; Margerine held the cigarette at arm's length over the match and did not put it into his mouth until half of it was in flames.

Fong was glad to see Margerine as he was once glad to see Fakhru. The conversation with the Chinamen was getting nowhere. He asked Margerine how his family was getting along, how the beer was doing and whether the bananas were ripening. These were the safe topics of conversation: Fong thought of the country privately as "Bananaland."

"Just this morning I gave fifty shillings to the Party," said Fong.

"What's the sense?" shrugged Margerine, puffing and then squinting through the smoke. "The Prime Minister—that monkey—has locked up five of his cabinet ministers. These ministers are all Dada and as you know the Dada people are the most fierce and primitive *savages* [he said this in English] in the country. There will be too much trouble, sure."

"We wait and see," said Fong remembering the milk, the paint, the unmade sign.

"What is there to see? Just more trouble," said Margerine. "Remember in nineteen fifty-six when the Queen came? A nice lady, the Queen. We were all happy. Then in sixty Philip [he pronounced this Philipy] took the flag down; bye-bye, I said. I felt like crying. All my friends were happy. We're free, they said. I said to them, you *buggers* wait one year and you will be crying too." Margerine shook his head and looked at his cigarette; he squeezed out the glowing tip, put the butt inside his rags and went out.

The Chinamen had watched it all with respectful awe. "You speak that black language?" asked the taller one.

"Oh, yes," said Fong. "I can even sing hymns in Swahili."

"That man is your friend?" asked the other.

"They're all my friends," said Fong. "When you're a grocer even one enemy is too many." Well put, he thought.

The Chinamen were impressed. "That is very good, you know. We have a little present for you." The taller one reached into his briefcase, took out a pile of books and magazines and placed them on the counter. "These are for you, Comrade. Read them. If you want more we will gladly provide them. Show them to your friends, our black brothers. In any case, we shall come back and talk to you. You have no idea how great your country has become."

"There is going to be a lot of trouble," Fong said. He had such conviction in his voice that the two Chinamen began speaking at once.

"That is a filthy lie spread by capitalist lackeys and war-mongers!"

"The dogs in America say that! Do they know that spindle production has risen three hundred percent in the past six months?"

"I am sure there is going to be trouble. I've been hearing rumors, and just this morning I was forced to pay. . ."

"Don't believe a word of it!" shrieked the taller one. "Don't worry, Comrade, these rumor-mongers are paid by American dogs and cats. Chairman Mao just last week swam fifteen miles—now you stand there and tell me there's trouble!"

"Chairman Mao?" Fong frowned. "I don't know about

Chairman Mao. I mean this country." And he added in Swahili: "Bananaland."

The Chinamen smiled, patted the magazines, reminded Fong that he should read them and noiselessly left the store. Outside, one turned to the other, and without moving his lips said, "Talk about lackeys!"

Fong put the magazines in the window and yelled again for Soo. She was in back pulling the wings off grasshoppers. She appeared at the doorway.

"What about the sign?"

"We have no paint," said Soo. "If you gave all the money to the black boy with the big stick then we have no money either. How can we buy paint?"

"I'll write a check," said Fong.

"But we have never before taken money out of the bank."

"Let me worry about that," Fong said, smiling. He took his checkbook from inside his shirt and wrote a check for two shillings. "Go buy some paint," he said, "quick."

# 10

Sam Fong was not alone on Uhuru Avenue. It was the longest street in East Africa and crammed with people and shops. Take an average day, average except for the worried-looking Chinese woman running from the lower end to the junction, dodging idlers and paper sellers, with a check for two shillings inside her dress and her hand flat against her dress holding the check in place as she runs. She runs slightly stooped, her feet slapping against the pavement; it is clear from the inexpert running and the number of people she bumps into that she is not used to running on the Uhuru sidewalk. A side street, perhaps, but not the main street of the capital.

At the lower end the street is narrow, pitted with ant caves; near the junction at the center of town an island begins abruptly in the middle with a broken KEEP LEFT sign, with palm trees, flower beds and people squatting or sleeping on the neatly trimmed grass. One fellow is roasting corn cobs over a charcoal stove. Those who live on Uhuru Avenue see nothing—they sell, they sleep, they haggle on the sidewalk, they buy one newspaper a day and ignore the stack of literature that is yellowing and curling upon the sidewalk near the paper seller. Only the tourists notice the completeness of the stack of booklets: *China Reconstructs, Yugoslavia News, Soviet Woman, Key to Your Stars*, the suitable-for-framing hand-colored portraits of President Kennedy and Patrice Lumumba, pamphlets of Gujarati love songs, *Machines That Made America* (Students Edition), *Peking Review, Reader's Digest, Ebony, The God that Failed*, J. V. Stalin's *The Foundations of Leninism* and V. I. Lenin's *Imperialism; The Last Stages of Capitalism*, these last two both low priced and austerely printed but nonetheless suffering the effects of being too long in the sun and dust; comic books with John Glenn in a space capsule saying "We did it!" and two-color pamphlets showing gross-booted Negresses smiling in Red Square and many more, all unsold, doing nothing more than drawing attention to the smudged daily, the typeface askew, the captions reversed but the headline still legibly exulting *COUP IN ALGERIA!*, while beside it and beside the inflammatory literature the paper seller slumps in a cretinous doze (his gaping mouth could be mistaken for a smile). There are people hurrying by who have better things to do than read: they are on twenty-minute coffee breaks, pocket-picking missions, they are begging and buying; and one, no longer yellow in the bright sun and seen only by those she barges into, is off to buy a can of paint.

In twos the whores march out of step wearing extravagant wigs wisped and spun with jet black horsehair mounted high and looking like charred beehives; their protruding bottoms bulge shiny against their bright dresses which, decorated with swirling metallic patterns, sparkle in the equatorial morning sun. They are the only ones who look at ease on the sidewalk; they alone are not hurrying; they ignore nothing, no one, take long, patient, undisturbed looks at men racing the engines of their cars at stoplights or men in shirt sleeves shielding their eyes from the sun. They are trailed by little dirty boys who nudge each other and imitate the girls walking. The high heels, the tight dresses and heavy purses of the girls give them a strange halting gait that is half ass and the rest purse as they clomp along Uhuru to the walkdown bars. What is oddest is that they are not black—their faces are brown mostly, some are quadroon yellow like that man alighting from the plane in the skin lightening poster in Fong's shop; the Congolese girls have long lateral scars on their cheeks, the Sudanese have symmetrical rows of bumps across their foreheads, others have claw marks raked parallel to their eyes. As they walk along they pat and adjust their wigs. Under their wigs their heads are shaven.

New to this crowd the Chinese woman pushes past two of them, and one of them smirks; it is a big, deliberate smirk and it takes up nearly one whole side of the girl's face.

The Chinese woman dashes past the National and Grindlay's Bank where resting Hindus take refuge on the shaded wall, symbolic meeting place for a thousand Asians on an East African Sunday afternoon; past the now green statue of George V, crowned and hugging a scepter to his robes streaked with birdlime; past the basket market and six ladies wearing (as they were directed by a brochure) simple, comfortable, low-heeled shoes, sensible dresses, roomy cotton brassieres and stupid-looking straw hats; past Cashco, the only supermarket in the country, air-conditioned to a dull chill seasoned with the dust of imported packaging; past the Mercedes agency where twelve lion-bearded Sikhs are goggling at their turbaned friend behind the wheel, his bracelet clanking on the dashboard, his dagger stabbing the upholstery, all bumping turbans and saying *yah-yah!*, and one African quietly, corpulently kicking the tire of a huge new model and inquiring, How much is that in shillings? She goes past a jeep loaded with soldiers who are giggling at one of their number who has chosen to amuse his comrades by aiming his air-cooled machine gun at passing cars; past the trophy-laden windows of the safari outfitters, two tusks framing rifles, bullets, bush hats with leopardskin sweatbands and one grinning head of a stuffed lion; past a *Wir sprechen Deutsch, Nous parlons francais, hablamos espanol* curio shop with zebra handbags, reedbuck rugs, ivory Christs, Zanzibari chests, legs of waterbuck made into lampstands, hoof ashtrays, elephant-foot wastebaskets, lion-tooth rosaries, hippo-tooth brooches; past six coffee shops, three of which have Hindustani jukeboxes and so have a score of Pakistani boys combing their hair in front and tapping their pointed shoes to the screech and clang of the latest hit from Karachi; past a bar which intrudes onto the sidewalk with men hunched in circles around little tables, each table holding the quart beer bottles of whichever race that table happens to be occupied by: Italian contractors at one, Greek bakers at another; two dark-suited Africans and a bespectacled American in native dress—flowing robes, rough sandals, an elephant-hair bracelet, a broadsword—at a third, semi-integrated table; five Englishmen, each wearing white shoes, long white socks, white shorts and white shirts and sporting pink faces and big ears at a fourth table; Indians sipping orange squash at a fifth, and so forth; past LAL SHETH TOOTH MAKER, FAZAL ABDULLAH KITCHENWARE, BOMBAY BAZAAR NICE TEXTILES; past RAHEMTULLA FUNSTORE, filled with slot machines and Africans, FANCY PANWALLAH, filled with betel nuts and Indians, NEW GOA GROCERY, filled with Goans and groceries and managed by Lobo who refused to buy Fakhru's canned milk. Uhuru Avenue is now a two-lane thoroughfare, with men in rags, and some not in rags, snoozing near the trunks of the palm trees planted in a row down the grassy islands; while the Chinese woman, who has not yet blinked, crosses the island and dashes in front of a dozen quickly-braking cars lurching around her, and into a side alley to MEHBOOB PAINT SUPPLY where, four years before, she had gone to buy the paint she needed for her first sign.

She points to a small can. It is handed to her by Z. F. R. Mehboob. She pulls the check out of the neck of her dress and smooths the little check flat against the counter. Z. F. R. Mehboob smiles at its smallness, mutters "Two bob only," wraps the can of paint in an old newspaper and jerks his head sideways in thanks.

The Chinese woman is out flapping down the street as Z. F. R. Mehboob hands the check to a small boy to deposit.

Down the main street she goes, faster than she came, past the palm section, past the section that was paved for the Queen's visit, past the post-Independence sidewalks—useful most of all to the beggars who now have a curb to sit on, and, as a bonus of progress to this city in a now different Africa, something entirely new, alien at first, but now serving necessity's perverse demands: a gutter.

All is blurred to the woman; she sees nothing because she knows she has no business on the street, she does not belong there and yet she knows she is running full tilt through color and noise, unseen herself possibly except by beggars. And at the far end of the street, she begins to slow down at the section without sidewalks, home of HASSANALI FAKHRU ENTER-PRISES LTD., ALI BUTCHERY, J. H. PATEL DRYGOODS, some tin-beating Africans in a vacant lot, a bar with no doors, a prostitute with the face of a pangolin leaning against a wooden shack, the taxi-rank, a quagmire of battered Volkswagens. Now she is panting, the can of paint in her hands, and she enters the last shop of the street with a gasp.

# 11

"INDEED," FAKHRU WAS SAYING, "HE CAN BE VERY DIFFICULT to deal with, but if you will excuse me for saying so, I am sure something can be arranged . . ."

Fakhru was at ease, he was happy and he was about to express his willingness to help. These feelings of generosity were inspired by the Americans who had done nothing more —but indeed it had taken them nearly a whole day—than follow the Rule Book and learn to say Fakhru's name. They cared. Fakhru was ready to help and had a feeling that, with his generosity, he could make a little money on the way.

Bert and Mel cocked their heads closer and tried to follow the Ismaili in his description of Fong. They had sent the office boy out for beer, but Fakhru had refused it; they had each offered Fakhru a cigar, and Fakhru had turned down the cigars as well, politely; Mel, who made a practice of putting the refused cigar in the man's pocket and saying "Keep it for later," discovered that Fakhru's pajama suit had no pockets. In frustration Mel went to a cabinet, took two fistfuls of Kents and dumped these in Fakhru's large soft lap. Fakhru did not smoke but said he would give them to his cousin who did. "Course we got no bidnis givin 'em to ya, but a body can't buy Kents *nohow* these parts," said Mel, and this caused Fakhru to smile and say thank you a third time.

Unbribed and looking reasonably comfortable in the chair, Fakhru continued to talk: about being brown in a black country; how His Highness had said this or that; how he himself, a humble tradesman, saw Africa as a test of his devotion, like a long exile with the usual temptations and hardships, as the Prophet himself had endured in the desert. East Africa could be a jolly place, he said, but—and here Fakhru looked frankly at Bert Newt—something had to be done with the blacks.

Bert said that scads of just plain vital little Africans had gone to the States where they had verbalized all their conflicts *vis à vis* the new developing nations in transition; the flap and feedback had been very good, generally speaking, although Bert said that he could not be more exact because he was not near the figures.

Fakhru shrugged and produced another smile. He went on, "And this yellow man Fong . . ."

There was a series of barely audible clicks in the room.

His tongue working behind his teeth to produce some very thick *p*'s and *t*'s, Fakhru warned the two men who were now anxiously nibbling at ball-point pens that they might have trouble understanding the curious language that Fong spoke and that, in any event, Fakhru himself would be glad, "more than heppy," as he put it, to act as interpreter. When Bert replied that they were ass-deep in liaison men Fakhru asked if they knew Swahili of the up-country variety. No, they said, they didn't, but added that they were sure someone did and thought privately that this someone, whoever it might be, could always use a little extra money; it was a poor country. Fakhru lectured them on the difference between Swahili as it is spoken by the devout on the coast and the kind uttered by the *muntu* trader a thousand miles inland. (This adjective made both Americans very uncomfortable.) Fakhru said he knew both kinds. Bert Newt, to shake off his discomfort, said, "Chrissakes, there are two kinds of *jambo*!"

Fakhru moved on to Sam Fong; he said that although Sam Fong had said he wanted to be friends, there were few people Fong trusted and this seemed to be a characteristic of the yellow race: they were excessively difficult to know.

"Thass puttin it mahldly!" said Mel.

"You can say that agin!" said Bert.

Bert had a feeling that the whole approach might be misunderstood. He assumed a kindly look and spoke out of the corner of his mouth, like a farmer, or at least the way he heard the farmers in the movies talk. He wanted to get to know everyone, he said, on a face-to-face basis. Of course they had scholarships, cultural exchanges and what-have-you for African students; but nothing, it seemed, could put them in touch with the grass roots, as it were. "Your average grass-rooter is a tough nut to crack—takes a lotta finesse to know 'em good," said Bert. Sam Fong was a good man to know, he knew "Your Average African," and Fakhru knew Fong. "We just wanna be friends," said Bert. "Who cares what color he is? Life's too short to start fretting about colors." He wagged his head.

"Amen, brother," said Mel Francey.

Sam Fong, thought Fakhru. He had never in his life seen two men so eager to do business. What did this yellow man have that they wanted so badly? Did he possess some great secret? Was he a criminal on the loose? Fakhru reflected and as he did Sam Fong ceased to be a man; very soon he became, in Fakhru's mind, a valuable commodity, like the UNICEF milk or free fly spray that had to be taken over and given a price, hustled out of the country and hawked to Sudanese farmers in order to be fully appreciated and used. As long as these things were free—like Sam Fong staring at the open doors of his shop from behind the far counter, like the milk or fly spray being tossed free of charge off donated trucks to tribesmen who hardly cared and who did not pay—as long as these were free they were without importance; they had no value and would fail precisely because they were gifts. Since people of different colors could never be friends, there could never be anything like an exchange of gifts; there had to be trade, and this commerce could be as meaningful as love. That was the way life went on. If this was never mentioned in the Holy Koran it was not the Prophet's fault, for he never had a family to support.

Fakhru grew silent and meditative; Mel Francey rose, winked at Bert and slipped out the door.

When Mel was gone, Bert looked at Fakhru and said, "See, this here's a great little country and we want it to stay that way. You remember what happened when the Chinese invaded India? Must have broke your heart . . ."

Bert continued. Fakhru repeated, "Of course, of course" at intervals and thought to himself: This bloody man thinks I'm a bloody Hindu.

" . . . And the same thing could happen here. Why I've seen it happen with my own eyes in a slew of other countries." He drew close to Fakhru and said, "Confidentially, it's happening right next door . . ."

Fakhru tried to think which of his friends owned the shop next to Bert's office. He could not think clearly so he smiled, looked at Bert and said, "In brief, as I understand it, you want to chet with my yellow friend, Sam Fong."

"That's all. No reason to get long-faced about it. We'll just debrief him a bit and shoot the bull."

"I must therefore warn you that he is, as you say, stubborn as a jeckess. He might have to be, as you say, helped along . . . somehow . . ."

"We're all human," said Bert. "I mean, Jesus Christ!" He laughed instantly and very loudly and then stopped. In embarrassing seriousness he continued, "See, this thing is my headache. I got your peri-urban minorities to deal with. Mel, he's your African man, your nationals; he's the right color, if you see what I mean."

"Of course," said Fakhru. "But the yellow one . . ."

"You let me worry about him. You think he'll talk really . . . ?"

"As I say, he might need, as you say . . ." Fakhru produced another smile.

"Yeah, yeah," said Bert. "But I want you to know one thing: you're swell to help us out here."

"I try my best," said Fakhru.

This was not the end of the conversation. Though Fakhru would have been very happy to leave, his politeness forced him back into his chair, and he added what he thought were appropriate remarks. Bert talked about Africa again, in general, and then about America's role in it. Fakhru was growing irritable; he had not had his morning tea and now it was almost lunchtime. He knew he would gorge himself on curry and *dal* and then want to sleep. Another day would be gone with only the beginnings of a very uncertain transaction made. He heard Bert say Africa a few more times and when Bert paused, Fakhru suggested that Africa was filled with monkeys.

Yes, Bert agreed, he had gone to the game parks with his whole family; he had seen them. He proudly pulled out baby pictures which he showed to Fakhru, very slowly and with many comments. In the background of every picture was a different facet of American life which, along with the weight and age of the baby, he described to Fakhru: a car, a typical house, a strong tricyle ("they don't come any better"), a set of golf clubs and so forth.

"You have an abundance of children," Fakhru remarked.

"No, I don't," said Bert, "only one, but he's healthy as a horse!"

"You have an abundance of sneps, then," said Fakhru.

"Yeah, sure, lotsa pictures. But it's the same kid." He smiled fondly at the snapshots.

The morning was gone. Fakhru was now very angry; he had had a dozen things to do and was not even sure if he had done one of them—who could understand what these Americans said? Fakhru made up his mind that if it was the yellow man Fong that the Americans wanted, then he, Fakhru, would put his best efforts into selling him, at a reasonable profit. And at the moment, Fakhru's hunger was so strong, his boredom so intense, he felt that the Americans would have to pay a high price for him. The British were right; Americans really didn't have any manners. He watched Bert Newt rise and he resolved again to make him pay; that's all he would understand, that's all any white man would understand: money. It was the only reason Fakhru had not gone out in a rage earlier in the discussion as he often did with Africans who squandered fortunes and hoarded trifles; like, though the comparison hurt him, his own children to whom money was nothing and a little green worm was treasure. He had no patience with them either. It made Fakhru sick to see people misuse money. Yes, that was the only reason he stayed; with men who seemed to know so little about Africa, the profit was sure to be great. The published fact that the living prophet, H.H. the Aga Khan, not only had many stables of race horses but also owned vast tracts of Europe and America as well, was of great solace to Fakhru. One had to be realistic in matters of money, and the Americans would soon learn the wisdom of paying and making others pay.

Bert put his arm around Fakhru and led him to the door. He started saying, "I want you to know I think you're really swell . . ." But Fakhru's face was ashen and Bert felt his Khoja friend go limp.

Over the door was a picture of the late President Kennedy. It was a good photograph: his perfect teeth, the knot in his tie out of place enough for all to know that he was just like everyone else, basically; his lovely brushed hair, the easy smile of a man who knows what he is doing, the face that all can love, young, even handsome, not unlike that of His Highness.

"Jeck," Fakhru blubbered with emotion.

Fakhru's face remained ashen, his eyes cast up at the late president. His blubbering died to a sniffle which he trimmed with his sleeve. But the tears continued to flow from his cast-up eyes, down his gray cheeks to his loose shirt. He removed his round beaded cap and held it chest-high, slowly squashing it in his grief-stricken fingers.

"He was a great man," said Fakhru still sniffling. "A great *bwana*."

"Yep. Sure was," said Bert Newt sadly, making wet noises with his lips as he stuck and unstuck them in his own grief. Bert did not know what to say. Like so many Americans, he was rendered helpless by death or great emotion. It was not a coincidence that the astronaut who was shot to the brink of the stratosphere in a giant rocket, gasped and said into his radio as he gazed—the first human being to do so—at the twinkling mystery of the universe, "Wow," was an American, like Bert. The death of the great prince made Bert helpless and sad, all the more sad since—like all the millions of others who stood mute after the murder was performed—he knew he had to be mute because now there was no one he could call on for help.

"Everyone loved him. It was a real love, for he was kind man, good man, honest man, and too young . . ." Fakhru did not know what to do. He felt it would be rude to leave, and yet the man, the American at his side, as if anxious to leave, had released his grip on Fakhru's shoulder and was shrugging silently and digging his toe into the carpet.

For a brief moment all Fakhru's anger was gone; his strong desire to cheat Americans was gone; no longer did he wish to help the Americans swindle Sam Fong (or whatever it was they planned to do). For a few seconds, before the picture of the late president, Fakhru achieved absolute peace: he loved all men and saw the wisdom in death, and giving without asking why, and begging in rags with a wooden bowl, and he saw the gift of innocence in all African countries, simple people who must never be harmed. Goodness illuminated all his thoughts, and such a glow, such radiance, that no man had a color and all men were equal and good. And goodness was continuous until the end of time because man was and God was, as the Prophet truly said.

Then the moment passed. Outside, traffic moved noisily down the street, there were yells, a sound truck with loudspeakers played a party song and somewhere in town someone was counting a large square pile of worn but negotiable hundred-shilling notes, wetting his brown finger in a sponge and making the old bills snap . . .

Fakhru replaced his beaded cap, and without glancing again at the portrait said, "Cheerio, *bwana*" to Bert Newt. At lunch Fakhru told his own assembled, munching family how the late President Kennedy came from a humble and wise, but extremely wealthy and shrewd family.

# 12

"You have chitted me!" shrieked Z. F. R. Mehboob. He began running feverishly toward Sam Fong's *duku*.

Africa makes her visitors very nervous, for it is only her visitors who do business, and business entails dangerous postures. Z. F. R. Mehboob's private fantasy of Africa was of a vast, a mountainous dark sow, bristling with old hairs and with a multitude of dugs for her piggies. She slumbers; the sun beats down on the piggery; from afar others come to suck. With a yawn and a groan the dark sow rolls over the sucking piggies. Some survive; those that do get very nervous, and understandably so.

Z. F. R. Mehboob came to Africa a quiet man, gentle in all ways, generous, given to prayer and impulsive acts of goodness. Four public declarations of bankruptcy and a near-revolution (the sow rolls over her farrow), the presence of black people everywhere that never smiled at him, turned Mehboob, in eight years, into a rumor-mongering bundle of nerves and a Persian. He was a Moslem South Indian; but the

77

kinship between Dravidian and Negro was too close for Mehboob to bear and literally overnight he became a Persian.

Eight years in Africa had refined Mehboob's techniques of raving and taught him courage. Now he would quite shamelessly run out of his shop and rave on the sidewalk, something that was not normally done by members of the Asian community. Shopkeepers and their families were seldom seen outside their shops. His wife, for example, only went outside the shop on Sunday afternoon to sit for one hour on the wall in front of the National and Grindlay's Bank; she was always accompanied by ten other women. But raving took no courage in Mehboob's eyes.

Typical of what Mehboob considered a courageous act was his monthly drive up-country to sell wholesale goods to bush *dukas*. Nothing extraordinary in this, one might suppose. But Mehboob had dreadful thoughts as he drove up the narrow mud tracks lined with high dense elephant grass: naked warriors watched him, savages who, if so inclined, could crush him. These fierce men were at the summit of every hill, behind large boulders which they could roll onto his van, his goods, his head; it was said that these tribesmen slept in the warm mud puddles in the middle of the road, indolent prey for the passing "Persian" who, when caught at the next village for the murder of the tribesmen would pay the maximum penalty, a punishment verified by his half brother's friend's cousin, a cotton-ginner in Burundi at the height of the Bahutu uprising against the Watutsi. The punishment consisted of cutting off the offender's feet and ordering him to stand on his stumps (raucous laughter as he falls), then cutting off his legs to the knees and making him stand again, and so forth . . . It was too much for Mehboob to think about; only the thought of it made deep dread. Mehboob considered the seven million Africans around him to be capable of it, but still he made monthly trips up-country in his van, alone except for his servant who rode in the back; he felt that at any moment he might be dismembered or crushed. Enemies were everywhere (sometimes pygmies stopped him by gathering in droves on the road—they beat on his car and sang until he agreed to buy a few poisoned arrows); even taking into consideration all the craziness that courage involves, and all the paranoia that the Asians in East Africa were heir to, some threats were real: a trip up-country was an act of boldness.

Raving on the street? Yes, although Mehboob did not think it very serious, even that required some courage. And here he was, Z. F. R. Mehboob of Mehboob Paint Supply shouting in a shrill Madrassi voice, "You have chitted me! You have chitted me!" to the blue African sky, uncluttered by clouds. He dashed, as the day before the yellow lady had noiselessly dashed, the length of Uhuru Avenue and into Sam Fong Friend Frocery.

Sam Fong greeted him with a nod and a grunt.

Z. F. R. Mehboob rushed up to Sam Fong and almost burst into tears; his face contorted and for a few moments he thumped the counter and was speechless. Then he shrieked, "You have bounced a check at me! You are a yellow thief!" This was repeated in Swahili.

"I have done nothing," said Sam Fong in Swahili, in order to clear himself and also to signal the fact that he could not understand Mehboob's accusation in English.

"Is chitting me nothing? Do you think I am a *mshenzi* fool? I am a poor man, my friend! And you have chitted me, you thief!"

"I pray for you to stop shouting in *Kizungu*," said Sam Fong, now distressed. He had seen Indians get excited before; he had seen one go mad and act like Mehboob, accusing everyone in sight of horrible crimes. Fong did not take Mehboob seriously; he simply wished that Mehboob's brothers would show up and drag him off as, fifteen years before, that other Indian was dragged into the bush and beaten insensible by his brothers until he became manageable enough to send to Calcutta. Fong made a new proverb which in its rough state ran something like "Never listen to the madman, but watch him closely."

When Soo Fong entered the shop Mehboob showed his teeth and snarled in the censorial way that dogs do. This angered Sam Fong but he realized that Mehboob did not know what he was doing. He folded his hands and asked Mehboob what he wanted.

"So you want to know why I came? Oh! If you would be so kind as to look at this please!" said Mehboob, mixing pleasantries with hysteria.

Mehboob took some scraps of paper from the folds of his clothes. There was Sam Fong's check, apparently uncashed. A little note was pinned to it.

"This is your signature?"

Sam Fong looked at the check. How inferior his signature looked in English; how lovely it would have looked in Chinese: two bold characters, each like a painted jewel box.

"Yes. That is my name. Sam Fong."

"Read this." It was a note pinned to the check; the name of the bank was printed at the top. There was a typewritten message centered on the sheet.

"Soo, read this paper," said Fong.

Soo took the paper. First she read it aloud in English, barely moving her lips, ". . . Leglet there are insufficient funds in the account to pay the above . . ." She translated the sad phrases into Chinese.

"I am a pauper," said Fong in a whisper.

"I want my two shillings and I want it now! If I don't get it I will ring for a constable or the nearest *askari* and you will end your days in prison." (Mehboob pronounced his last word "brison.")

"I had almost shillings seven hundred only in my bank."

"You have nothing in your bank now. You have no bank!"

"And there is no money in the store," said Fong, violating his proverb, listening and believing instead of just watching the madman. "The young boys collected all my shillings from me to give to the government. I have sold nothing for two days. We are eating locusts again. If what you say is true, then I am a pauper, I have nothing . . ."

Z. F. R. Mehboob wailed again, agonizing, throwing his head back; this wailing after a few moments turned into plain dry baying.

Sam Fong looked up at him. He was sad. Madness in an

acquaintance is unpleasant, but one's own poverty is unspeakable; it means indignity and an inauspicious death.

Fong was wondering whether he should throw himself at Mehboob's feet and beg for mercy ("I will ring for a constable") when Fakhru walked in. Fakhru saw Soo Fong in the corner, the dirty-faced children peeping around her legs and holding to her long skirt; he saw Sam Fong, silent, with folded hands; he saw his friend Mehboob face upraised and baying at the empty top shelves.

"I greet you all. *Salaam*, Mehboob," said Fakhru. "What is the *monena*? Are you unaware that quite a large crowd has gathered outside to listen?"

"My check for two shillings has bounced *kabisa*," said Fong.

"Calm down, Mehboob," said Fakhru placing his hand on Mehboob's shoulder. Mehboob stopped baying and faced Fakhru; his eyes were red and his jaw was slack.

"I am robbed and you tell me to calm down!"

"To be robbed of two shillings is to be blessed," said Fakhru. He took two shillings from his purse and placed the coins in Mehboob's hand.

Mehboob looked disappointed; his whole face relaxed into regret. He had made up his mind to be offended. He felt doubly cheated. He had been eager to continue baying. "No Persian would stand for this insult," he grunted, feeling the money. "You may tell the yellow one that if he sets foot again in my store he will be asking for a beating." Mehboob left, snarling and pushing his way through the crowds of Africans that had gathered at the entrance.

"Your check bounced?" asked Fakhru.

"Yes. Only two shillings and I do not know why."

"Have you forgotten the one you gave me?"

"Yes. No."

"That one did not completely bounce, let us say. But you are in my debt for shillings three hundred and seventy only. This includes Mehboob's two."

"It is true. I am pauper."

One tear ran out of the right eye of Soo Fong and down her cheek.

"What are we going to do?" There was no emotion in Fong's voice; he meant what he said. For the first time in many years—almost since the time, thirty-five years before, he had walked to Foochow with rags on his feet and eaten an occasional rat—he had nothing. What was left on the shelves would not keep them alive. One does not eat aspirin and skin lightener and grow fat. The situation was desperate and because it was desperate Fong could not afford the expense of getting excited, of beating on the counter and weeping until another crowd gathered. He appeared very calm. But the words he was speaking to Soo in Chinese were of darkness, poverty, slavery, humiliation and, without resorting to ambiguity of proverbs, death.

Soo Fong said nothing. There were several more slow tears, but no sound came from her lips.

Fakhru seemed to understand. He waited until Fong stopped speaking in Chinese (Fong had not turned his head; he appeared to be praying to the empty air in short lunatic syllables), and then leaned forward and said, as sympathetically as he could, "I think you should see the Americans."

# PART TWO

# 13

Fong's guess was correct. The Young Pioneer who had dropped into the grocery store to extort money from him *had* been a bad sign, like the obnoxious winged demon in African superstition who shows up in a person's head shortly before a tragedy and flaps foolish signals that only a witch doctor can fathom. The Young Pioneer never came again; no one came to the shop for a long time. There was trouble.

The Prime Minister, as Margerine had reported, had thrown out more of his cabinet ministers, all Dada. They had been criticizing him, people said. They were fed up, one high official was reported to have said. One of the cabinet ministers had been seen in town, drunk, saying that the country was bankrupt; no one had actually seen or heard him, but many heard that he had been seen.

The full story of the dismissals was told to Fong by Margerine. It ran as follows: The Prime Minister invited all his ministers to the State House to discuss the rumors. ("Let's be English about this," the Prime Minister was supposed to have said; to the press he said, "Mind your own business. This trouble it is just a family squabble because I am fed up of this disloyal and stupid cabinet.") When the ministers arrived and were seated and drinking in the mansion the army drove up, handcuffed six of them who were pointed out by the Prime Minister—a careful sign from him, perhaps a gentle nod— threw them into the back of a truck and took them to a detention camp.

At the moment of his arrest, one of the ministers (he happened to be the Minister of Finance) suddenly produced two fistfuls of American dollars from beneath his traditional costume (long robes embroidered with lovely designs, and a peaked cap that made him look like a sorcerer). He waved these two crumpled bouquets at his colleagues while frantically repeating that he had lots more for anyone who would help him. He was seized by three soldiers. The remaining cabinet members pretended not to see him until the trucks were out of sight. Then they made a dash for the money that had been knocked out of the Minister of Finance's hand. This they divided equally.

It was a simple operation, the six arrests, and this might have been the end of it had the whole affair been kept as quiet as the Prime Minister requested it should be. But one hour after the last minister was tucked struggling into the back of the army truck, rumors began to fly about town. That was when Margerine told Fong the story in detail, breathlessly, glancing around as he whispered.

In each shop on Uhuru Avenue a similar scene took place: the owner of the shop listened carefully to the worried whisper of an African ("It's their country," said Fakhru to his wife. "They should know"); the African, in return for the information, gratefully received a free cigarette which—since it had to be smoked in the presence of the shopkeeper—extended the story of intrigue and allowed the African to add details of the arrests as well as a bit of background material, tribal wisdom and warnings. Sam Fong and the Indians closed their shops. Those that had iron gratings locked them across the plate glass. Trash barrels, bicycles and laundry were brought inside. The streets were deserted, empty in the sunshine.

The rumors were contradictory. But the existence of rumors indicated that something was seriously wrong; it did not do any harm to close early and take a holiday and stay off the streets. The rumors each started off truthfully saying that the ministers were taken to the State House to discuss a problem of national interest. At this point truth lapsed and fantastic savage descriptions took over; these descriptions may have indicated to a certain extent the sincere wishes of many who were spreading the rumors. The dominant story was that the ministers had been tied up on the floor, their hearts cut out by the Prime Minister and his chef and these organs distributed to the remaining ministers—some of whose teeth *were* in fact filed to sharp points—who ate slabs off the still pulsing things, for strength in battle. One rumor had the Minister of Health washing them down with the blood of one of his former colleagues. Other rumors told of the ministers roasting on spits, tortured with heated spears and disemboweled. And there were many hints of sexual violation. The news on Radio East Africa said nothing of the arrests, but listed a number of people going on courses to England; the major news item was of a man in New Jersey who had a plastic stomach grafted to his innards, the point of the story being that in his old, ulcerous stomach-sack two buttons, some paper clips and the U.S. equivalent of fifteen shillings was found.

When the rumors reached the relatives of the luckless ministers some of the relatives had their lawyers prepare habeas corpus briefs to be submitted to the courts and others paid nocturnal visits to witch doctors for medicine strong enough to destroy the Prime Minister. Other relatives of the arrested ministers gathered in groups to begin sabotaging the government. This last alternative was by far the most popular. It became even more popular and more violent when the government passed a law in Parliament (this was two days after the arrests) making it illegal to carry weapons and a criminal offense to spread rumors. Old ladies with bundles of firewood in their arms were arrested for possessing dangerous weapons; several men with walking sticks were charged with treason, attempting to overthrow the government by force. As soon as rumor-mongering became a criminal act rumors began in earnest and everyone was now firmly convinced that the ministers had been killed and devoured, with relish, *in camera*.

The terrorist gangs blocked roads and tore up hunks of pavement, pulled down power lines and beat up tourists. They roughed up twelve Germans so thoroughly that the Germans, who were by no means of slight build, were rushed shrieking to the hospital. The German Ambassador's picture was in the paper the next day gloomily pointing to twenty-six broken cameras. The government said that this incident proved that the arrested ministers deserved to be in jail; their constituents and henchmen had no regard for human life or anything decent. In the meantime, an English tea planter was hacked to death, an up-country surveyor's wife was sexually outraged by three men and a rural sociologist was set upon and his glasses smashed ("Your goggles are finished, ha-ha," the attackers said, according to the sociologist). The terrorist gangs worked busily, efficiently; it was almost as if it had been planned months in advance. They beat up a few Africans whom they called "stooges," burned a few grass huts and then with methodical passion began breaking the plate glass of Indian shops and tormenting the Asians. One Indian girl was raped with such insistence that she had to be sent to Bombay on the morning plane. In protest her father closed his shop and said he would never open it again. Many Asian boys were stripped naked and made to run home. If silence can be taken to mean a certain deep understanding, the Asians seemed to understand perfectly why their community was being attacked. For the time being the ministers were forgotten.

The rumors now said that it was all part of an Asian conspiracy to take over the country and outbreed all the Africans. The little Indian girl that had been raped and sent to Bombay was accused of enticing Africans to sleep with her in order to get information from them; caught in the act she had screamed to make it look as if it was defilement instead of sabotage. She lost all African sympathy and the next day the Asians suffered a renewed attack from larger numbers: more shops were broken into and looted; two were burned to the ground; the flower beds of Uhuru Avenue were trampled. Fakhru and his family moved into a cement room at the back of the house. Sam Fong nailed his children into a packing crate and he and his wife rolled themselves into reed mats where they stayed for most of the day, like pastries. Detail was added to the conspiracy rumors: the Asians, it was said, were breaking into their own shops, burning and looting them so that they would win the sympathy of the government which would in turn punish the Africans; at the same time the Asians would be collecting insurance on the damages.

The government did nothing. From time to time statements were issued saying that no rumors should be believed and that anyone who believed them would be dealt with severely. The Minister of Information said on a special radio broadcast that he had heard many rumors to the effect that people were believing rumors and spreading lies that he personally was satisfied were untrue. He further implored the Asian community to calm down and not to cause any further disturbances. Nobody had anything to worry about. He explained that really nothing had happened, no one had been arrested—certainly not the cabinet ministers; the whole misunderstanding was the fault of a few rumor-mongers and "some people who don't mind stealing and sucking blood from the Africans, but aren't men enough to take out citizenship because they don't have any guts at all . . ." The broadcast finished with the Minister of Information saying over and over again and even into the fade out, "Things are back to normal, I tell you. Things are just back to normal . . ."

This was followed by more attacks on the Asians. Fakhru looked down from the window of his cement room and pleaded with the gangs of boys to stop breaking his windows. "Why are you doing this to me?" he moaned. "Because you're not having guts," was the answer. Sam Fong suffered no damage, but he remained in the back room rolled in a reed mat with his eyes shut just the same.

Then mysteriously the attacks stopped. Mehta explained this by saying that since all the stores were empty and there was nothing more to loot, the Africans were merely giving the Asians a little time to stock up with more merchandise from Nairobi. When more goods arrived there would be more stealing, he said. But this was not the reason. To Mehta one terrorist looked very much like another; in fact, each arrested minister had his own terrorist group, and the terrorist groups had now started to ignore the Asians in order to effectively terrorize one another. They continued in this for a week, until one group had subdued all the others; with the help of the groups that had been subdued, the dominant group directed all its rage against the government. The terrorists broke windows of trains and cooperative societies, raided police stations, tipped over a bus, broke into several schools and destroyed equipment, burned down the house of one minor politician and raped another's wife.

The army was called in. The army was composed almost entirely of one particular tribe, loose-limbed, tall, muscular men with purplish skin, graceful necks and small, closely set eyes. They had a loping, pigeon-toed gait and handled their rifles like walking sticks, now clumping them on the pavement, now swinging them, now pointing them—all done with simple-minded ease and great strength. Their lips were genially everted, their heads perfectly formed—rounded in every plane—and their ears were small, tightly rolled and very delicate. Although they were widely reputed to be cowards, most people had seen at least one soldier bullying or beating someone, and no one openly defied the soldiers.

In a very unsystematic way the soldiers began appearing in bars and on the streets; they leaned against the posts of shop verandas and sat sullenly in doorways. More than one white housewife gliding through the supermarket searching for a broom handle came upon these large armed men idling near the Coke machine at the back, their rifles with bayonets fixed resting against the kitchen utensils. On a dozen curbstones the soldiers sat, rifles across their thighs, their legs sticking out in two directions, their heads lolling over heavily in sleep. The presence of the soldiers caused considerable alarm—it was more than their size, their purplish faces, their uniforms, it was, in fact, their submachine guns. In a country with little experience of armies it is fear rather than anarchy that is inspired in people who see soldiers among them. To be anti-military is a complicated reaction for a naked man facing an armed man. For the naked man to be scared out of his wits is simpler and, from the government's point of view, more convenient. The terrorist groups faded out of sight. The soldiers were offered no resistance; the Asians opened their shops and joshed them with generosity.

COTTON PRODUCTION UP 1000 BALES THIS YEAR! or TRIBAL CLASH IN TOGO or U.S. TO BUILD SCHOOL OF DOMESTIC SCIENCE were the headlines in the newspaper. No deaths, not even the presence of the soldiers, was mentioned. A State of Emergency had been declared the day the soldiers appeared; the announcement was made once and never repeated. The Asians sat in their shops behind shuttered windows and watched the empty sunlit avenue. The shelves were bare. Africans began drifting into the streets. There was now a fatigued panic, a disordered anarchism which showed itself as totally aimless drunkenness, casual abuse and fistfights that ended abruptly without a victor as the fighters suddenly dropped their arms and walked away. It was an orgy of not caring that even the Minister of Information was unable to soothe, directed against no one, purposeless, hardly serious and almost not harmful.

It was at this time, a month after the arrest of the six ministers, in this period of shambling chaos, that the Prime Minister gave one of his sermons. He came in convoy to the main stadium; in front were the motorcyclists waving people off the streets and stopping traffic; behind the Rolls Royce were truckloads of market mammies singing party songs and chanting his name over and over in singsong. The melodies of the political songs were those of hymns; the words had been altered. One, to the tune of "Moses Hath Deliver'd Us The Promised Land," had been adapted by substituting the name of the Prime Minister for Moses and Af-ri ca for Pro-mised Land. The Prime Minister carried a fly whisk and a cane and wore a three-piece suit. His bodyguards and his mistress accompanied him to the platform where he sat glowering through dark glasses at the audience squatting in the dust. As he rose he lifted his arms and his jacket was removed; the cane and fly whisk which he casually released never hit the platform floor: they were caught by cabinet ministers to his left and right, and returned. The Prime Minister belched into a lace handkerchief and began speaking over the slow chanting of his name. He spoke with many pauses so that the translator at his right could convey the message in the vernacular. The rings on the Prime Minister's fingers glittered as he spoke.

"Brothers!" he shouted, "God has seen fit to make me your Prime Minister and I thank His Great Wisdom and Mercy for giving a humble man this chance of a lifetime! I am a simple African. You are simple Africans. Your parents and their parents before them were simple Africans. Your children are simple Africans. We are all Africans. Africans are black, unlike Englishmen who are white. We think as Africans. We play and work as Africans. I speak to you as an African when I say unto you, God has seen fit . . ."

Sam Fong sat with his whole family, seven yellow, sallow people, small and neat, almost lost in the grandstand in the sloping pudding of black nationalists and rags. He had been awakened at five that morning by a Young Pioneer who ordered him to go to the stadium at once; and there Sam Fong sat for four hours, waiting for the Prime Minister to show up. Neither Sam nor Soo nor the children stirred; they tucked their hands up their sleeves and hunched over. Their faces were turned without expression upon the Prime Minister who continued to shout "Brother this" and "Brother that" and to repeat his black incantation whenever he seemed at a loss for words. The translator had a high voice, it was almost a screech; he shook his fists and bounced on his toes and at the end of long sentences he asked for applause: "Now *clap*!" The audience clapped.

The speech contained very few different words, but the words were said over and over in many patterns as if they were not part of a speech at all, but rather magical syllables which became weighted with more magic in their repetition.

The Prime Minister said, "Poverty, ignorance and disease are our greatest enemies" five times; then he said, "I say unto ye the ministers I arrested are nothing but stupid enemies and skunks." For "skunks" there was no word in the vernacular; he changed this to snakes, for which there was a word. After this he repeated "poverty, ignorance and disease" several more times, amid cheers, and followed it with an appeal to the Young Pioneers to find every disloyal citizen and bring him to justice for punishment. Yells from the Young Pioneers assembled around the platform encouraged the Prime Minister. He said that from that day onward the Young Pioneers would be his personal spies ("I baptize you *The Black Guards!*" he shrieked) and that everyone—including the Asians, the vandals and the troublemakers—would have to step lightly.

He said that perhaps he would be accused of being too harsh. He didn't care. "I'm not going to play second or even third fiddle to the Chinese or the Yankees . . ." No one understood Africa, he said, even Winston Churchill didn't understand Africa. ". . . And sometimes even I, an African, do not understand Africa! So are you going to turn around and tell me that some stupid fool who isn't even black is going to tell *me* about Africa? I was in Chicago, Las Vegas, Wales, Rome, Waco, Texas and even in Frisco, and I didn't tell anyone how to run their affairs. I kept my big black mouth shut . . ." There was an uneasiness in the audience, the applause had gotten noticeably less and there was a slight murmuring; the Prime Minister quickly began speaking in a very high voice, dropping definite and indefinite articles, with a bush accent: "I am not communist man, not even democrat or fascist man. What do these *kizungu* words mean to me? As you jolly well know, we all being simple Africans from dirty villages. Communist and democracy these are big words from big book. What are book anyway I ask you. These things they call book are just crushing out our brains to hell . . ." There were loud cheers. The crowd was won over. It was as if he had crooned them a song.

"No, I say unto ye, I am African and I am Prime Minister and God help the false friends who try to overthrow me—I

will throw them straightaway to the crocodiles!" The Prime
Minister sputtered and shook his fly whisk at the audience:
"Now you know there has been a little family squabble down
at State House. Pay no attention to it, don't worry about it,
don't think about it. Go back to your banana groves and be
quiet; plant more seeds this year, use fertilizer. I warn you that
if you get mixed up in this unhealthy business, what I call
family squabble, you will not live to squeeze your handfuls of
porridge. This is especially a warning to our friends the
Asians . . ."

As the Prime Minister said these words a thousand brown
men in the stadium stiffened, closed their mouths and allowed
their heavy lids to droop. During the next part of the speech
these men appeared to darken a bit, go browner. Even Sam
Fong, who was sitting very near to the Asian section, seemed
to become unmistakably swarthy as he listened.

"I will say this only once and I hope your ears are wide
open. We will not tolerate people who smile and then go
ahead and take money out of our pockets. This is what I call
cat and mouse friendship because you're running with the hare
and hunting with the hounds and I hope that is abundantly
clear especially, I repeat, especially to our very good friends
the Asians who had better walk on tiptoes from now on . . ."

The Prime Minister accepted the applause. The Young Pioneers—"The Black Guards"—were not sure whether they
should stand to attention to show how well disciplined they
were or whether they should cheer and sing to show how
much they loved the Prime Minister. About ten stood still; the
rest whooped and hollered the Prime Minister's name. The
Prime Minister flapped his fly whisk at them and left the stage.
The entire audience stayed at rapt attention while the last part of
the speech was translated into the vernacular. It was difficult
translation. There were no words for pockets, cats, hounds
and tiptoes, just as a bit earlier there had been no word for
second fiddle. When the translator finished (with considerably
less hyperbole in his words)—the Prime Minister had long
since driven away—it was clear to all the Asians that the
crunch was coming and that they were being held responsible

for the family squabble. They filed out of the stadium in groups of ten, for safety. Sam Fong joined the Asian groups not so much because of the safety they offered, but more because (this thought made him very tired) he was a debtor and he felt obliged to follow them, at a decent distance.

# 14

Sᴀᴍ Fᴏɴɢ ᴋᴇᴘᴛ ʜɪs sʜᴏᴘ ᴄʟᴏsᴇᴅ. Tʜᴇ ᴊᴏʙ ᴏꜰ ʙᴏᴀʀᴅɪɴɢ ᴜᴘ ᴛʜᴇ windows gave him enormous pleasure: a whole platoon of the army could not have broken through those neatly sawed and joined boards. He fed his family on food from the cans. He did not really want what was in the cans, but they had rusted, the labels had mildewed and they were unsalable: the cans of Spam from Minnesota, the processed cheese from Melbourne and the shiny unlabeled cans which, without emotion, Fong discovered to be tomato juice tasting strongly of steel. Sometimes at night, as he huddled with his family in the back of the boarded-up store, he heard the *pop-pop* of gunfire. It was a small noise, like a firecracker, and not the cannon noise he had imagined it would be. He also heard voices, again just mumbling voices, small, not screams; he heard people running down the street, their bare feet slapping on the pavement, and then the sound of boots and heavy puffing, a voice, *pop*, a sigh—none of it loud or even scary, but more like the sound of a radio playing a thriller two large rooms away.

The noises were not loud; their ghostly smallness did not frighten. Yet it was clear to Sam Fong that he should not go outside or answer the door after dark. These long nights in the ripe dank of the store, in almost dead silence, caused in Fong a religious fervor that was awakened slowly, as the nights passed, in oddly shaped memories. He was like a man piecing together a long silent dream. He recognized it as fervor immediately, but it did not become religious until the memory was nearly complete. He stopped telling his children stories of the Emperor and the rice paddies and the streets of Foochow that were crammed with rickshaws. There were no more stories like the one he had told of the tiger he had once seen in a thick cage, near his village, guarded by a black Indian who, for rice and meat, would bang on the bars of the cage with a stick and make the tiger open his mouth wide. There was once astonishment, even savagery in his stories; now there was a gentle solemnity. Fong told about little Jesus helping his father in the carpentry shop; the murder of the innocent children (not bloody; it was their souls which mattered and these ended up in heaven) by the bad King Herod who wanted Jesus but never found him; the guardian angels whose wings ("Bigger than that counter there") protected all those who loved God. Fong told his children the few Latin phrases he could remember and the way to say the rosary. They said the rosary, fingering the beads, ten Hail Mary's and so forth into the long night until, with the muffled sounds of the people running and the *pop-pop* of those in pursuit outside the strongly boarded shop, they all dropped off to sleep, their rosary beads still clutched in their hands.

There was another story that Fong had lately become skillful in telling, also religious in its way, the story of a search. Fong squatted on the floor, his back straight, his small hands raised making quick gestures as he spoke. It was about a man who left his family and wandered through the world, across the ocean and desert and in the dense banana groves; he was punished by fearful winds and storms, by black people, brown people and white people, by earth rumblings and wild beasts. God sent these things to him because the man did not understand them; God wanted to make sure the man was sincere and good—good enough so that he could finally love what he did not understand. Sometimes the man almost gave up, but when he remembered that it was God Himself sending troubles to a very little man he realized that there was order in the earth. At the end the man was poor; he was very upset and almost broken, but he did not lose his faith. He triumphed because he was in a strange land and he knew how to be patient and how to pray.

With this new fervor Sam Fong passed his nights peacefully with his family and was so engrossed in his piety and gentleness that he did not notice how short his supplies were getting. When he finally realized this there was almost nothing in the store: there were some onions, there were two unlabeled tins, there was a handful of rice and perhaps a pound—if one included their inedible wings and legs—of grasshoppers. The cans of milk were there in crates, but for Fong they did not represent food; he did not drink milk and he discouraged the rest of his family from doing so. The cans, furthermore, did not represent the promise of money, for the shop was closed and there was no telling when it could open. Standing in tall piles, gathering dust and harboring roaches, the crates very rapidly became a symbol of helplessness, for his piety calmed him but it did not fatten him, and now he was nagged by hunger. The children cried easily and it became hard to tell them even a simple tale. There was no money, not even a halfpenny. Soldiers shuffled on the street. Fong took a mystified look around the dark, boarded-up shop; what seemed most strange to him was that so much time, so many years could have passed and now, old, with children scuttling around his ankles, in his closed grocery store he had a dumb lonely vision of all those years in Africa.

The vision was foreign, plainly odd rather than shocking: he lacked what the Chinese call "the necessary grains"—he had nothing; he was among neither friends nor strangers, but enemies; and worse than not owning anything, he was himself owned. This last thought almost made the meditation painful, but when Fong recalled the story of the man who was sent great suffering he reached the conclusion that only very few are sent great suffering, and pain is a blessing when it is sent by God. Fong knew it was a gamble which in a moment of weakness he could lose completely; everything could be gained as well if he were strong. Another look at the empty shop, now buzzing with one underfed fly, and it came to him again: *I have nothing, I am owned, I am a slave in a strange country.* Fong remained in the grocery store and prayed. His prayers were pure: they were praises; they contained no threats, no requests, no bargains; they asked nothing and offered everything.

Fakhru was all smiles and had his son by the throat. It came to him that he was thoroughly enjoying throttling the little boy, that it was doing him, Fakhru, a lot of good. He let the boy drop to the floor. He rushed away in a rage of disappointment. Earlier in the day he had been on the verge of stabbing his houseboy (the houseboy was against the wall, Fakhru's knife was very close to his ribs, having already pierced the front of the houseboy's uniform), but reason prevailed: he kicked the houseboy in the shins and was done with it. He knew he would be hanged (he, a civic-minded person with a sense of values and fair play) if he stabbed the houseboy (a dung beetle, a man to whom a kick was sound advice, a black man *and* a Christian). The houseboy had dropped a cup. Fakhru's son had said that someday Africans and Asians would marry each other and when they did there would be no color difference: Africans would lighten a bit, Asians would get darker. Fakhru had not hesitated a moment. The thought of his empty unprofitable shops, the Prime Minister's speech about "playing cat and mouse" and picking people's pockets had removed the domestic pretense of Fakhru's patience, that slight pause of natural politeness before insult was uttered. He wrapped his fingers around his son's small neck and a thought came to him which he said aloud: "You are an Asian because I am an Asian, and you are my issue. No one cares about us because we are Khojas and know the value of a shilling. If I kill you no one will care, no one will hang me, for you are an Asian. I am doing this country a service by ending your brown life. The Queen might give me an M.B.E. . . ." He smiled; he was not excited, he spoke calmly, realizing that he could rid the world of one renegade and not be blamed for it, and as he spoke, smiled and realized this he tightened his grip and squeezed harder. Shortly after, he dropped his little boy and stopped smiling. The boy's color was now green, but he was alive and rubbing his neck. It came to Fakhru that he had tried to kill two people that morning and it was still not time for lunch.

He clasped the photograph of H.H. the Aga Khan and held it before himself so that he could see the face of H.H. framed by his own puffy, sweaty jowls mirrored in the glass. He loved the tragedy of it: the brooding red-eyed Fakhru tormentedly showing over the serene Aga Khan, bestower of good will, with soft doves in his breast. I must calm myself, he thought; I can't go around attacking the houseboy, my own family. He looked at the young Aga Khan and had two quick thoughts: one was *He has very white teeth which means he does not take betel*, and the other was *Does he know what a trial these blacks are*? He thought of the Prime Minister's speech, of the empty shops—*his* empty shops—and winced. The blacks were getting restless; he could be asked to leave the country tomorrow. In a couple of hours he could be sitting in the dust, penniless in Pakistan or wherever the blacks shipped him. He had thought of this before—scores of times. He knew he could be deported with no warning at all; he also was well aware that, forty-one years before, he was born in a country which now he had no memory of. Fakhru complained incessantly of Africa, like Mehboob, but he knew it would be deadly to leave. He was prepared to leave, however, and assumed—as most of the Indians did—that he would be on the plane for Karachi or Delhi the next day.

It is always prudent to buy off one or two of them, Fakhru thought, and then he quickly reconsidered. He would give them nothing: Bribes are expensive, I am a poor man, I may even be a madman, but I am not mad enough to give away my money to these monkeys! The doleful perspiring face contin-

ued to stare out from behind His Highness. Fakhru thought
again of his own property, now idle, not earning a penny; he
thought of the many rents which, because of roadblocks and
soldiers, could not be collected; other stores burned, looted of
all merchandise. The thought of rents and shops and things he
owned brought him to Sam Fong. From there it was, mentally,
a very rapid transit to the Americans.

Mel Francey had taken to calling them "Injuns." "What the
Injuns up to today?" he would inquire of a shopkeeper. Or,
"You Injuns better keep your heads down for a bit," he would
say in discreet warning. After the Prime Minister's speech, all
of which was recorded on the spot by Mel's and Bert's secret
abdominal tape recorders, Mel had said, "Them pore Injuns
gonna get their raggedy asses kicked straight out of this
place!" Mel had not made up his mind about the Asians. He
knew they were dirty and threw things on the lawn and did not
eat with their left hand for a very good reason; he was quite
sure they swindled Africans, but—and this was the real problem—he did not know whether he had made up his mind
about the Africans. He was not crazy about the Africans; he
found it hard to say two words to them without them asking
for a free trip to the States, and recently he had noticed that
the Asians laughed good-humoredly when he squeezed their
hands, winked and said, "What's new with mah ole pals the
Injuns?"

Mel went to the window. The orange dust was rising in a
cloud as a dozen fully armed warriors with bells and feathers
and leopardskin loincloths jogged toward the Nile Villa Hotel
where fifty Rotarians from Cedar Rapids—on their way
around the world—were expected to be lunching; old men in
short pants languidly pedaled their bicycles; urchins played in
the bubbly filth of open drains. Mel felt odd; he was in a
foreign country, away from home.

Being away, that was a new one. He used to think of Africa
as home. The previous year, his first, he had stood in the very
same (air-conditioned) spot and looked down; he had just arrived from Washington where, at the airport drugstore, he had

been racially abused by a drunk in overalls: the man had called him (he winced inwardly) a "no account coon." But Mel's own inner resources, coupled with the knowledge that he was going to Africa, and, more than that, was an Afro-American, helped him to be tolerant and walk away from the man and, with dignity, board the plane for East Africa. He had arrived in Africa—it had long been a dream of his: Mel Francey, Afro-American, good-will ambassador, in his own sweet land. Louis Armstrong had done Ghana; James Meredith, Nigeria; Cassius Clay, Egypt; Martin Luther King, Liberia; and Mel Francey, East Africa. He had, that year before, looked down at the people shuffling slowly on the baked and littered African street, one of the first main streets he had ever seen with rocks and boulders strewn on it, and said to himself, *these are my people*.

That ended. A new feeling (it used to be cruel but recently had stopped being cruel and become dull) was of remoteness and being among strangers. He did his job, an easy one; it merely required his vigilance and a surrender of will, and when he did think private thoughts he thought of Alabama and being away. Even in his worst persecuted moments, when he felt what he was doing was obviously wrong, a betrayal, and that he should get himself back to Mobile and quietly sit at the front of a bus with his eye peeled for those who might call him an "uppity no account coon," even in those awful moments he did not look at the tangle of sleepy bodies ambling down the street and think, these are my people. A year before he had, but that year had changed him, eliminated the sentiment and made him a perfect stranger.

He seemed to be dozing off until he saw two figures dodging the tiny cars in the street (everyone had a small car; the cars were like little toys). One figure was clothed in white and wearing a beaded cap and wide flapping trousers; the other was small, wore a white short-sleeved shirt and a huge cork helmet. Mel got his binoculars out of his desk and peered at the two men. It was them, they had come.

Relief was one of the sensations Mel felt when he saw Fakhru. This was unexpected—the feeling of relief, not

Fakhru. (Fakhru was long overdue: the State of Emergency had interrupted what Mel thought would be a fast contact.) It was as if, in the middle of all the East African heat, he felt cool ginger ale materialize in his mouth. The State of Emergency, rumors of a coup, a countercoup and soldiers deserting by the hundreds, atrocity stories ("You won't believe this, but they took this little girl . . ."), and, especially retailed by the American community, the stories which began "When I was in Uttar Pradesh . . ." and ending "Boy, it was touch and go for six solid months," had punished his patience and fatigued him. What upset Mel especially and often made him angry was that his colleagues were fond of telling him about what they called "your African." "Your African," they would say, "according to your best authorities has this tiny little gland that squirts smelly juice over his skin to scare your moskeeters away. And man, your African has a shit pot full of aggression and no more sense of decency than a hound dog . . ." Mel could not help but feel that it was not the granddads in short pants, the warriors and pygmies getting their pictures taken by Rotarians or the scores of gland-secreting terrorists who seemed to drop, silently in droves, out of the trees at sunset when everyone locked himself in his house; no, not "your African"—they weren't talking about *him*. They were talking about Mel, and he didn't like it one bit. Not only was it the stupid and thick-headed racism in the statements that he knew so well and despised; more than that, each statement indicated plainly that Mel (and family) were no different from those people down there on the street, pissing against the side of the National and Grindlay's in full view of everyone; Africans, whom he had grown to dislike so much. He was just like them, the color kinship, that's what everyone thought, and he was getting damned tired of it in a quiet way which he expressed only in sighs.

Fakhru and the Chinaman paused to let a car pass. Mel put down the binoculars, dashed to his desk and buzzed Newt. He returned to the window and saw the two men enter the building. Mel felt relief. He was worthwhile and doing his job; he was of some account; he had scored.

"Now how's mah ole frins the Injuns?" said Mel when Fakhru and Sam Fong were seated surrounded by free cigarettes, Pepsi-Cola ("Your Moslems are by and large teetotalers," the chargé d'affaires had said; he had spent a little time in Cairo), copies of *Why Vietnam?* and, safely out of their wrappers and tubes, some Havana cigars.

Fong was tense. He sat uncomfortably in the huge chair, his cork helmet in his lap, his feet dangling, not touching the floor. He was hunched over, unblinking, attentive and uncomprehending, as he had been at the Prime Minister's rally, as he had been indeed ever since he lost his job at the carpentry shop in the Ministry of Works. He glanced at Mel and Bert from time to time, but kept his eyes mostly on Fakhru who giggled, clucked and tilted his head in affirmation and respect. At intervals Fakhru asked permission to translate into Swahili ("I will put our yellow Chinese friend into the picture, please"): "You see, these Americans know their business," "It is a nice place—free Pepsi-Cola and everything," or "They are going to start talking business any minute now..."

"Let me put it this way," said Bert, coming to the point after twenty minutes of how hot the weather was, how it was muggy, just like Baltimore in the summer. "Does he know what the score is?"

"Most assuredly," said Fakhru, "but as I have perhaps mentioned before, he wants to know exactly what it is you want him to do."

"Reason we ask," said Mel, "is that we want him to know that we're behind him all the way..."

Fong looked at Fakhru and gulped audibly to call attention to himself. Fakhru turned and said, "Negotiations proceeding well. We will proceed slow-slow. Quick-quick makes bad luck." To Mel he said, "My friend understands you but does not wish to comment. These are hard times. We are beset, if I may say so, and are suffering dearly—blamed, I would say —for the present unrest. Many of our shops have been broken out of and our community has been attacked by His Excellency, the Honorable Prime Minister. These harsh words and also sticks and stones. Sticks and stones may break our bones, but names will never hurt us, as the noted proverb has it. It is the stones which worry us greatly indeed thank you please."

"Sheer thing," said Bert. "But your average newly independent country goes through your usual . . ."

"Many of our number have disappeared, many injured. An abundance of shops burned. My windows broken. Sheth's daughter molested and sent to Bombay."

". . . phases of growing pains . . ."

Mel sighed.

"Yes. Well, life is not without peril. We hope for the best. But, if you will allow me to say so, my fellow friend has undergone deep tribulation and humiliation. His modest grocery shop has been plunged into ruin by the present state of affairs in which the blacks are killing each other, not to mention members of our own community. My friend Fong's business is finished, *kwisha*."

"Washed up, eh?" said Mel, but not kindly.

"Yes, please. One might put it that way."

"You tell him he doesn't have a thing to worry about," said Bert. "Understand?"

"They are being difficult," said Fakhru to Fong. Fong looked at the Americans.

Bert grinned at Fong and nodded his head, and exaggerating the words with his mouth hissed, "Yesssss, yessss, yessss." He also rolled his eyes as he hissed the words.

"What are they saying?" asked Sam Fong. He spoke his Swahili quickly; the Chinese intonation added a dull metallic note to it and so his sentence came out *cluck-cleek*.

"Patience," said Fakhru. "Leave everything to me."

Bert Newt coughed. "I mean, we're always glad to help friends in need. That's what makes the world go round. Last year foreign aid amounted to billions of dollars—*billions*!"

"Good heavens!" Fakhru exclaimed. "The yellow man Fong is in very great need. Poverty is a dreadful thing; it makes one lose one's dignified, well-being and estimation. Observe this poor damaged man. He is thin as a snake and quiet as a mouse. He suffers, you see. And yet, as I have told you, he is not an easy man to deal with. Perhaps this is why he has no estimation and is poor—because he is filled with stubborn." Fakhru looked at Fong with pathos; his own English was going to pieces; a *billion*, he thought.

Mel looked at Fong and saw only the enemy. Sam Fong threw grenades, sang stupid songs, made pig iron in his back yard, marched idiotically and held up a little red book called *The Sayings of Chairman Mao*, wore a shapeless wrinkled uniform with red stars on it and a cloth cap like Barney Old-field's. Sam Fong raped nuns on tables, burned pagodas and produced children like they were going out of style. He infiltrated and sabotaged African countries. Mel was getting edgy. Sam Fong, the Chinaman, had spoken only once, in Swahili; he was not responding to good will; he sat breathing slowly through his nose. He made Mel so nervous that Mel, a non-smoker, snatched up one of the Havanas, bit the end off and began chewing it unlit.

"Tell him we don't want anything from him," said Bert, wiping his mouth with his handkerchief. "All we want's a chance to do him a good turn."

"They appear to be giving in," said Fakhru to Fong. "Now we will eventually strike a bargain. They have a very wide selection of merchandise," he added brightly.

"I am your slave," said Fong. "I have nothing to say except my freedom from your debt is very important."

"You want to starve?" asked Fakhru.

"A happy man cannot starve. I was happy today until I remembered that you owned me."

"This transaction will make us both free," said Fakhru. "You free and me free."

Sam Fong blew a sigh.

"What did he say?" asked Bert eagerly.

Mel wheezed, crossed his legs, uncrossed his legs, bit his cigar, spat out some strings of tobacco and wheezed again.

"It is his habit to be difficult," said Fakhru. "He said that customarily one does not get something for nothing. Of course, I don't agree, but he says . . ."

Bert leaned over and said, "Tell him . . ."

"*Tell him to cut the crap!*" shouted Mel. "We get his ass

down here and tell him we want to be *frins*! We tell him fifty times we don't want him to do anything, just take our good will is all—and this is the thanks we get! Well, you tell him to *loosen up*, hear? Cause if he don't loosen up he can take all our good will and shove it!"

"Mel," pleaded Bert.

"I'm sick of this blah-blah-blah jive. Why don't he jess take our good will and forget it? Huh? Is it cause we too damned nice or what?" Mel slowed down. He looked at Fakhru. "Fakhru, I like you boy. You're a square shooter and you and me, we got something in common: you nowhere and I'm nowhere. But you tell this guy if he don't loosen up then I'm gonna jess write that bitch off as a loser . . ."

"What Mel means—and you can correct me if I'm wrong, Mel . . ."

"You wrong, boy," said Mel quickly. "You dead wrong! Now you let *me* handle this." He turned full upon Sam Fong.

Fong had listened to the outburst without moving; now he inched slowly backward under Mel's gaze, like a yellow cat who sniffs danger coiling up on a chair.

"You tell him *first* to cut the crap," Mel said now calmly, with reason in his voice. "Then you tell him we're not gonna pussyfoot around the place—no sir, not when we're fully prepared to finance his business and get him back on his feet and out of the red."

Out of the red, thought Bert. Good title for our report.

"You mean money?" One of Fakhru's eyes seemed to come unhinged. It lolled sideways.

"I mean *money*," said Mel. "What's the use of playing games?" he explained to Bert who was as stiff in his chair as Sam Fong.

The next exchange was in Swahili:

"I think we are making progress."

"What is all the shouting about?"

"They are simply listing the products they are prepared to sell us. And at a very good price. Too good."

"What's the word?" asked Mel.

"He is still reluctant. He wants to know what he is wanted to do."

"Tell him . . ." Bert began.

"Tell him he's jess yaller!" shouted Mel. And then Mel's expression changed: it glowed and widened; he laughed, too loudly, repeated what he had said and laughed again, and now his laughter closely resembled hooting.

Fakhru looked at Mel and Bert. Mel was still grinning and emitting hoots at greater and greater intervals; Bert was immobile and seemed to be in a state of shock. Mel's eyes were red; Bert's were glassy, pearly. Mel was loose, Bert starched. For the first time since he had entered the office Fakhru felt the moment was right for a move. The two men had eased themselves, one by shouting, one by silence, into a position where they were incapable of bargaining sensibly. Sam Fong did not have the slightest notion of what was happening. Fakhru made his move.

"The yellow man's business is very modest"—pause—"but it has big possibilities."

"Now thass what we like to hear!"

"He is a clever man as well"—pause—"but then so are we." Fakhru winked.

"Damn right," Mel winked back.

"Mmmmmmm," murmured Bert.

"They have a shipment coming in very soon," said Fakhru in Swahili.

"Who cares?" said Sam Fong.

"He is seeing it our way," said Fakhru in English.

"Now you're talking," said Mel.

"He is used to dealing with his own countrymen," said Fakhru. "He is unaccustomed to American generosity."

"We'll show him what America's prepared to do," said Mel.

"They have a lot of bleck market merchandise. *American* bleck market. Smile," said Fakhru in Swahili.

"I am your slave," said Sam Fong. He smiled.

"Now we're getting somewhere," said Mel.

"He wants a check," said Fakhru simply, in a small voice.

"Tell him to name his price!" shouted Mel with exuberance.

"*Mel*," said Bert. There was agony in his voice, but still he did not move a muscle; he said nothing more.

Mel put his face next to Bert's. "Look, Newt, you want this creep or don't you? Say so now or shut your fat honky trap." This came out in a hoarse voice that was intended to be a whisper.

"They are being difficult," said Fakhru in Swahili. "Nod your head up and down two times."

"Money enslaves," said Sam Fong in Chinese. He nodded his head up and down two times.

"Grin."

Sam Fong grinned and showed his bad, grasshopper-nourished teeth.

"Only fifty thousand shillings," said Fakhru.

"How much is that in *real* money?" asked Mel.

# 15

ONE DAY LATER, WHEN EVERYTHING SEEMED QUIET AND THE sun was shining on the thick blossoms that littered the island of palms on Uhuru Avenue, and only the soldiers gawking into store windows or ambling along in twos and threes indicated that something might be wrong, J. H. Patel, V. R. Gupta, Z. F. R Mehboob and a young man known as "Dino" Raheem were served with deportation orders and given twenty-four hours to leave the country.

The official statement to the press said that the four "acted in a manner that was disloyal and disaffected toward the government."

Fakhru learned of their impending deportations while he was standing in line at the bank, where he heard most of his news (it was the only place where he did not give someone a penny to stand in line for him). He knew the four very well; he had done business with Patel and Mehboob; Gupta was well known; and he had often seen Raheem combing his hair before shopwindows.

With the American check duly—even gladly—endorsed with Fong's signature, Fong thinking the whole time that it was not a check (it bore no tax stamp and was larger than the East African ones) but an invoice for American goods, Fakhru was almost as conspicuous in the bank as the deportees getting their last traveler's checks. Fakhru had three Nubian body-guards who wore flat World War I helmets, bamboo shields and wrist knives. They each carried a long spear, one a wrench, another a bayonet and the third a broadsword with half the blade missing. Except for their weapons they were naked. When the check was cleared Fakhru withdrew 25,000 shillings in twenties. His briefcase proved too small to hold all the notes. He asked the bodyguards to put some in their pockets; they shrugged and raised their weapons, exposing their sleek nakedness. The deportees, however, were settling their affairs in the next line; they were each allowed to take only 1000 shillings out of the country. Fakhru suggested they get their allotment in hundred-shilling checks, put these in their pockets and sell him their briefcases. To console them Fakhru said, "I am thinking that you will not be needing these anymore, especially if you are bound for our motherland." The briefcases were handed over. Of the remaining amount Fakhru deposited 300 shillings in Sam Fong's account and 24,700 in his own.

Business over with, his five briefcases bulging with hard bundles of new notes and his bodyguards hovering around him, Fakhru went to the Foreign Exchange counter where a large Asian crowd had gathered. He listened to the details of the deportations and offered his condolences.

Later in the morning Fakhru detoured over back roads to his house. He put half the notes into his safe and hid the rest in his mattress, behind the Queen's picture, in pots and pans and in between the pages of a number of holy books; then he hurried off to tell Sam Fong of the "first transactions," the 300 shillings and the unfortunate fate of the Asians.

The boards were still across the front of the grocery store. Fakhru rapped on the boards for several minutes before he realized that he was the landlord; he went around the back and opened the rear entrance with his own key. Inside, Fong and his family were crouching, pale and unarmed and expecting the worst.

"It's not the soldiers," whispered Soo in Chinese.

"Don't be so sure," murmured Sam Fong, eying Fakhru

"Brother," said Fakhru, "you will thank me in profusion when I finish speaking. . ." He told Sam Fong that he had during the night received and sold some American merchandise on behalf of the grocery store, and had deposited the money in Sam Fong's own account. "Not much, but slowly by slowly makes a big bundle, as our friends the Africans say." There would be more, of course, when "a few more details can be finalized."

"We have money in the bank," said Fong to no one in particular.

Soo screwed up her face. Then she got the checkbook.

Fong asked if he could write Fakhru a check there and then for a hundred shillings, "or is this a trick?" Fakhru assured Fong that it was no trick, that with things in the country as they were they had to stand shoulder to shoulder; he accepted the check and gave Fong five twenties which were passed to Soo.

Soo ran out of the shop to buy food. Nothing more was said between Fakhru and Fong until Soo returned, prepared the food and everyone had (ravenously, deliberately, chewing rapidly and not speaking) eaten. Belching into his empty plate —with disgust Fakhru had watched Fong lick it with his pink tongue—Fong said simply that he had not had solid food for a week. He was not complaining he said, and it did not worry him; not only was there a State of Emergency and no business, it was also Lent. "And man does not live by rice alone," said Fong.

"Most certainly," said Fakhru, thinking Fong had said "rent." He smiled, then told Fong what he had heard about the deportations. Fong listened with interest. Deportation was something that he dreaded; his overriding fear, above that of African violence, the occasional earthquake, the dry spells, paganism, new taxes, hot weather and the frequent changes of government—each new government arriving with screams, shooting and mobs of rock-throwing people—was the fear that he would be sent away. Where would he go? He had no idea. China, he felt, might not after thirty-five years be the same place. More than anything, Fong wanted to know the reasons for the deportations: "What kind of men are they?" he asked.

"Patel is a Gujarati Hindu from Baroda; Gupta is a Bengali, a Brahman, or so he says; Raheem is a Punjabi Muslim; and Mehboob, whom I had thought to be one of ours, a Khoja, Ismaili, turns out to be a Moslem South Indian, Dravidian perhaps, almost a *karia*, a black. But the minister says," Fakhru took out a newspaper and read, "'They are Asians, known for their wily ways and tight fists, and all are cut from the same cloth, in this case cheap Asian cloth.' Bad joke, I would say."

"No Chinese?"

"You are the only yellow man here, my friend. When a Chinaman goes, it will be you."

He is telling the truth, thought Fong. He pinched his face at Fakhru. Fakhru was being a friend. Sometimes he was an enemy. But friend or enemy, Fong still knew that Fakhru was the only man he could talk to, he was his only link between the grocery store and the world that lay outside his boarded-up windows. It had been that way for over four years. Sam Fong did not at the moment consider the fact that his debt to Fakhru was unpaid, that none of the canned milk was sold and that he had no choice but to listen to Fakhru and do what he was told. He was so moved by the act of kindness in recognizing that he too had no place in East Africa ("we have to stand shoulder to shoulder") that he completely forgot that he owed money and was virtually owned by the man in the pajamas, whose gob of betel juice was now running down the wall of his back room. He was a kind man, a brother; *no, not that*, thought Fong, *but kind, yes*. "What did they do to get deported?"

"They're not deported yet, not until tomorrow. They had been told to *bugger off*" (this was in English) "in twenty-four hours. You ask me what did they do? I will tell you. I know all of them very well . . ."

He started with J. H. Patel. Patel's crime was selling dry goods at wholesale prices to the sister of the Minister for External Affairs on unlimited credit. When the bill became large Patel visited the minister, but was turned away; the minister told him he was being greedy and that a white man would never come in and act that way. After the visit, the sister got more than ever in debt; the amount owed was now huger and more hopeless, the chances of repayment nil. The State of Emergency put an end to the sister's purchases—Patel's shelves were empty—but she had gotten so much merchandise from him that she had no place to store it. She asked Patel how much he wanted for his store. He said, "Why do you ask me how much when you know you have no money to buy it with?"

"You're just saying that because I'm an African," said the woman.

Patel protested. "No, I'm not a racialist. We are all brothers—even Mr. Nehru said that. But I am a businessman as well as a brother. I say you have no money because you have no money. You owe me shillings eighteen thousand six hundred forty-two only, which I know I will never see . . ."

The sister of the minister called Patel "a tightfisted bloodsucker" and said that she was going to tell her brother how the cheeky Asian had insulted her.

"Now Patel is leaving. The sister has two stores, lots of merchandise and no debts. Nice, you see?" said Fakhru.

Mehboob was the most innocent of all. He just happened to be noisier and more conspicuous than the rest of the traders; it was unfortunate that his shop was in the center of town where everyone could see him, but that could not be helped "because it was his father's and his grandfather's shop as well," said Fakhru.

There were various accusations against Mehboob. First, he was an Asian and therefore looked down upon Africans, the Africans said. It was also said that when he got drunk he shouted for all to hear: "When the Asians go, so does the economy! Long live *wahindi!*" He kept his daughter chained in the back while he "went about with African women who painted their lips and burned their hair." He made Africans drink from a cup which he refused to touch. (Fakhru explained to Fong that Mehboob did not even use his wife's cup because it was "unclean," and made his wife bathe before she prepared food.) The Africans said that Mehboob was discriminating against them; although he liked Africans, "We know what he is really thinking: he is despising us!" The head of the Young Pioneers said, "He thinks he's special! Well, we'll show him how special he is—we'll kick this rogue back to India!" Fakhru said that ever since the Prime Minister's speech in the stadium the Young Pioneers had been shouting this on the grass outside Mehboob's paint supply store. Even the police were getting tired of hearing the noise, and when they asked the Young Pioneers to stop it, the police were threatened with violence and told to mind their own business. To simplify matters and set an example, and also to keep the peace, the police decided to tell the government to serve Mehboob with a deportation order. "Easy, no?" said Fakhru

V. R. Gupta was a nationalist whom Fakhru disliked intensely ("If ever there was a troublemaker it is V. R. Gupta"). Gupta spoke four African languages and knew most of the tribal customs; he once alienated a roomful of Indians who were discussing the viciousness and chronic thievery of a certain Nilo-Hamitic tribe by saying quite simply, "It is because they are a pastoral people; agriculturalists are more concerned with property."

He was born in East Africa in 1906 and resembled a *sadhu,* bony and wrinkled, leathery but with a warm light in his gray eyes. Throughout the colonial era he had struggled to bring independence to East Africa. He organized and consolidated African opposition to the British colonial government; he let Africans use his back room as a secret office, started and edited a newspaper (later banned by the Colonial Office) in which nationalists wrote about how they only wanted to live and work together as equals and build a society for all races to share as equals and have a voice, and so forth. When the

Africans were jailed Gupta hired lawyers for them. He often said, "I was born in Africa. Africa is my home. I am an African..."

Fakhru did not think Gupta was in his right mind. Gupta *was* an African; that was the trouble with the little Hindu. He spoke nonsense ("It is because they are a pastoral people") and formed the first political party in the country, financed the party and advised the party leaders, who were all Africans, on constitutional matters. When the party won the first election Fakhru suspected that Gupta had a motive and was perhaps cleverer than any other Asian in the country; but Fakhru was tired of hearing him accuse the Asians of not cooperating with the Africans. "You will pay for this in the end," Gupta warned.

He did not have the majority of Asian support, but he had a great deal of sympathy: the land laws were discriminatory before Independence, only whites could own land and grow cash crops. But he made enemies quickly among members of his own community by saying, "In the eyes of the whites you are also black men." He had no desire to chase the whites out of the country or to terrorize them. He said that the Africans must have what was rightfully theirs in order for all the races to settle things lawfully and fairly. Mahatma Gandhi had been an encouragement to Gupta's father (the great man paid his father a visit on the East African coast at Lamu in 1893); Gupta himself had the personal support of Mr. Nehru; but in spite of the fact that Indian nationalism was an inspiration to him and his African colleagues, Gupta said, "When someone calls me an Indian my heart is heavy." Gupta was the first Indian to have an East African passport and said he was proud to be a citizen of East Africa. "In America aren't the Italian immigrants—I quote the late President Jack Kennedy—all of them Americans. So let us all be Africans..."

Three communities spat in unison at Gupta's suggestion. Gupta did what he could to bring the races together, but none would budge. Fascist sentiments, put forward as "realistic" by the leaders of each community, were agreed upon in a hapless sort of way by everyone except Gupta. Leading African businessmen saw Gupta privately and told him he was wasting his time; "Let's face it," these men said, "Africans *are* dirty, they *do* smell—I'm an African: I know. And they're happy where they are, isn't it?" Gupta sighed and attempted to reason with them. He spoke of the brotherhood of man. The British said, "Yes. Hm. We've got quite a mixed bag here. But masses of complications, if you see what I mean ..." The Asians repeated the proverb about its being impossible to take the curl out of a dog's tail, even if you bury it in the ground for weeks. The one time Gupta saw Sam Fong, Fong told him the Chinese proverb, in Swahili, of the monkey you could teach to ride a horse, but the monkey's hands were still hairy. And everyone went on buying and selling.

Gupta turned back to the government. He studied the parliamentary reports closely after each session ended. It was obvious that things were not going well (one member of Parliament suggested that a law be passed to limit the size of Asian families). Perhaps, Gupta thought, there was not a constructive and vigorous enough opposition. He saw value in his supporting the Opposition party: it was a legal party, the members seemed honest, their spokesmen only needed encouragement in being active in parliamentary debate. Gupta helped the Opposition to grow and at the same time saw it as a moral duty not to withdraw his financial support from the ruling party.

This was his mistake. Word got around that Gupta was masterminding the overthrow of the government through the Opposition party, so that the Asians and their African "stooges" could take over. All the back-benchers in Parliament were locked up along with the six ministers at State House. The imprisoned politicians were said to be in collaboration with "The Leech," as Gupta had come to be called by the government. The Prime Minister's speech in the stadium had been directed against Gupta; "the cat and mouse friendship of running with the hares and hunting with the hounds" was a reference to Gupta's support of both parties. Gupta was "disloyal and disaffected toward the government." There was documented evidence in Gupta's own handwriting to the effect that elections were a year overdue and it was "time to ask the common man, in a democratic manner, if he wanted a change of government . . ."

"Only troublemakers want elections," said the Minister of Defense.

Gupta surrendered his passport and agreed to leave the country within twenty-four hours; he knew enough of constitutional law to see that in a flash he had been made stateless.

"A fool, in other words," said Fakhru.

Sam Fong stared. He looked for a pattern in the deportations but saw none.

"Now Raheem . . ." Fakhru explained that Raheem would be a liability to any society. He had no job, but always had money "because he is in the habit of pinching tires and then selling them back to their owners." He slept with African girls and introduced a number of perversions to his circle of friends; he drove too fast, he chain-smoked and ate pig; he was indiscriminate in telling people—African, Asian and white—to fuck off. He had respect and admiration only for Americans, and his one wish was to marry an American girl who looked like Shirley MacLaine ("That broad has class," he said). Because he went to the movies every day he picked up a strong American accent and a number of slang expressions. His nickname, "Dino," was given to him by one of his own seedy admirers (he had a gang) one day when Raheem leaned against the fence at the cattle market, and, tossing his head in the direction of the Wambugu Fishnet Factory where many young girls were employed as stitchers on the machines, said, "At least we're where the action is."

He had started to believe that he was Dean Martin. He and his gang saw all the Dean Martin movies, and afterward, the members of his gang said, "You were super today, Dino." "Yeah," said Raheem, "they can't screw me." He did not have an objectionable voice. That day at the bank, while the mob of Asians told Fakhru the details of the deportations and got their traveler's checks, "Dino" Raheem looked at his reflection in the glass wall at the Foreign Exchange counter, and, ignored by the babbling Asians and tossing his head, sang:

*"It was just one of those things,*
*Just one of those cr-azy things,*
*One of those bells that now and then rings*
*Just one of those things . . ."*

And when he finished the song he turned to the Asian mob and said, "Okay, cats, let's get this show on the road . . ."

Fakhru confessed that he understood only Patel and Mehboob. Sam Fong said he understood none of them; he thought privately that if they could be deported, so could he. He thought of China: his village, the huts, the cows, the sun setting on the paddy fields.

"They're leaving today?" asked Fong.

"No. They have twenty-four hours. They're going tomorrow."

# 16

THE PRIME MINISTER WAS ALSO LEAVING. HE WAS GOING TO his farm to work in the soil, he said: "Planting has to begin even when you're a prime minister." He had to get his mealies planted before Parliament was called, "and my advice to all you *bwanas* is to forget about politics and do the same." But the general feeling of the Asians was that the Prime Minister was taking no chances and that several attempts had already been made on his life by supporters of the arrested ministers. Among the Asians it was whispered that the Prime Minister's "farm" was in London.

The Prime Minister's departure on the same day as the deportations was a stroke of luck for the Asian community. It meant that the Asians could go to the airport without being accused of saying good-bye to (and therefore sympathizing with) "the disloyal bloodsuckers." V. R. Gupta, "The Leech," was seen as especially dangerous, "a stoogie who should cast the moat from his eyes," as the editorial in the weekly of the ruling party described him. Any demonstration of sympathy toward Gupta was sure to mean trouble for those who sympathized. For twenty-four hours the Asian community practiced caution; they avoided Gupta altogether. His packing was done in silence, alone, in his office, the old *saddhu* shuffling among his tables littered with papers and the autographed pictures of well-wishers: African nationalists and American political scientists.

Fakhru persuaded Sam Fong that it would be very wise if he also went to the airport, "not to see these bloody *wahindi* leave, but to make the old man's departure more auspicious."

Fong did not see the logic in this. He reflected that there was rarely logic in these moves, or if there was he could not understand it. He could only ask God's guidance and large protective beard (Fong had thought from his earliest days that the faithful, the devout, were allowed to hide in God's bushy beard; this was simple because Q. *Where is God?* A. *He is everywhere*). What Fong had not considered was that Fakhru's offer had a great deal to do with the Americans. This was not anything very sinister on Fakhru's part; but Fakhru's friendly visit and affectionate bursts of betel juice on the wall of the grocery store were all prompted by his special deputation as guardian of Sam Fong ("Keep an eye on him. You take care of him and we'll take care of you, Fakra"). As he had agreed to this and accepted the check on behalf of Sam Fong he had to make sure that the Americans got their money's worth, that Fong became friendly, that his store reopened and prospered, that he was grateful to the Americans and seen regularly with Fakhru in whom the Americans had placed much of their trust and a good deal of their money. It was no effort for Fakhru to do this, for to keep Sam Fong at his command he knew he would only have to prevent him from ever being able to repay the 370 shillings that Fong owed. With Fong's shop closed this hardly required any effort; in fact, Fakhru realized that the danger was not in Fong's paying the money back, but rather in the strong possibility that Fong could very easily starve to death. By depositing small amounts of money in Fong's checking account Fakhru knew that he could keep Fong alive and in his debt until the end of time, and could please the

Americans ("Smile." "I am your slave." A smile). There was no logic in it, but there was a degree of order, and it was from this order, created by Fakhru, that profit was born. Fong did not see the logic because there was none; the fact of his debt to Fakhru kept him from ever seeing that his poverty had been ordered by Fakhru. If Fong had detected this he would have thrown Fakhru out the moment the first gob of betel juice hit the wall.

Fong agreed to go to the airport to see the Prime Minister off. Fakhru picked him up in the gray van; in the back of the van were the three Nubian bodyguards who were not only armed as before with knives, arrows, spears and the broken sword, but were now decorated with little bows (on the arrows, around their biceps, trailing from their waists in fluttering skirts) in the national colors: gold, red and black. The bodyguards peeped out from the back of the van as it drew up to the grocery store. Sam Fong got in front with Fakhru.

The airport road was jammed with vehicles—cars, buses, bicycles—and people walking in groups. It was a narrow road; many dangerous curves caused it to be called "the road to heaven." Even now, a full hour before the Prime Minister's departure and the deportations, several accidents had occurred. At Milestone Two a bicycle lay twisted in the road; twenty feet away the rider sprawled, his feet and one of his arms turned unnaturally back to front—like a dropped doll—his face against the street, flattened, glued with blood. Cars detoured slowly around the man. "When the Americans get to the moon they will find there a black riding a bicycle," said Fakhru as they passed the corpse. Farther up the road two cars had pulled off; the rear of one was crushed, the headlights of the other were smashed. Standing in the shards of broken glass were the drivers, smoking cigarettes and taking turns yelling. Sam Fong counted two dogs, a cat and four snakes squashed flat and seeping innards on the road, all delicacies, the whole lot (with rice and vegetables) enough to feed the average Chinese family for a month.

There were Asians in most of the cars, men in the front seat, women and children in the back; the rear window of each car displayed seven or eight heads of long braided hair gleaming with coconut oil.

Fong did not speak. He looked with regret at the dead cyclist and the squashed animals. Death upset him; he saw nothing more. A month after he arrived in East Africa he stopped seeing mud huts, women pounding peanuts in large wooden mortars and naked children tending cows, prodding them with long poles; he did not see the activity along the road, only the death, although the simple items of equatorial life, the activities of tribesmen, were all there unchanged, existing as they had existed thirty-five and even three hundred and fifty years before. Fong was startled by the screaming of the police sirens. About a dozen white-helmeted policemen on motorcycles roared beside the line of traffic, waving their arms and making gargling noises.

"He is coming," said Fakhru. And without another word he pulled off the road and came to a dead stop.

The cars in front did the same, pulled into banana groves and beside fruit stalls, leaving a wide corridor of road without a single thing moving on it. Five minutes passed and several police cars careened by; long black arms swung threateningly at the parked cars. It was against the law to be moving when the Prime Minister drove by. While they waited at the side of the road Fakhru told Sam Fong stories of people—mostly arrogant Greeks from the Congo—who had not obeyed this law and how they had been kicked by the police.

After eight minutes the Prime Minister himself, standing like Father Divine in a red open-topped Rolls Royce, his lion's mane fly whisk aloft and snapping in the breeze, zoomed past; the tires sucking at the hot soft tar made the only sound. Behind him were "his women"—in another Rolls—and behind his women were three truckloads of singing youths, the Black Guards and one busload of market women clapping their hands and singing the song about the Prime Minister, "who showed us the Promised Land."

The Prime Minister's procession was made up entirely of Africans; they stuck their knobby heads out of the cars and grinned when they overtook the parked cars, the Asians.

When the procession had passed, the women who had stopped pounding their peanuts lifted their heavy pestles once again; the little dusty boys resumed poking and kicking their cows; men in doorways tilted gourds of beer up and took long swigs; radios were flicked on; and out of the fruit stalls, turnoffs, driveways, side roads and banana groves wheeled the Asians, gunning their engines and roaring back onto the airport road, swerving and jockeying for position among the cows and goats.

The parking lot at the airport was full. Fakhru, however, merely hunched over the wheel pretending he was one of the Prime Minister's functionaries. He followed the Prime Minister's procession to the front door of the main lobby where he deposited, for all to see, Sam Fong. One of the bodyguards, at Fakhru's signal, opened the door for Fong and stood, helmeted and armed with a sword and covered with colored bows (but otherwise naked as a jaybird), while Fong clambered out and winced at the large crowd.

"I will join you straightaway, my good fellow," said Fakhru in English for the benefit of the people standing near the Fakhru Enterprises Ltd. van.

Sam Fong shrugged and ducked into the crowd that filled the lobby. The Prime Minister had entered a few minutes before and was in the V.I.P. lounge making a statement to the press about the necessity for using lots of fertilizer on the tung trees this year. One journalist asked him about the deportations and he replied, "I don't know a bloody thing about these deportations. I am a simple farmer, I tell you." Fong was being crushed; he fought for air and wriggled through the crowd until he saw an empty space near the weighing-in counter; several Asians milled around near the counter showing passports and exchanging Hindustani words in soft voices.

Above the murmuring of the crowd in the lobby burst one angry nasal voice; Fong listened but did not understand a word of it.

"Tell these gringos I don't dig people pushing their lousy mitts all over me!" said an Indian in a pink shirt, pointing a comb and sneering at two huge black policemen.

The angry Indian with the comb stalked over to another Indian at the counter who looked at an air hostess, his mouth set in a grin of pain; the air hostess said that he would have to weigh his camera. It was J. H. Patel. He looked at her, held tight to his camera and said nothing.

"Hi, you little pastafazool, how's yarass?" said the Indian with the comb, rolling his eyes at a small, sleek, Indian girl standing at the edge of the crowd, her eyes downcast; she adjusted her sari on her shoulder and continued to stare at the floor.

"Yes, I am J. H. Patel. That is correct, I am being deported. You will observe my British passport," said the Indian with the camera, still grinning in pain at the air hostess.

"Let's hit the road, Jack," said the Indian with the comb.

"My name is not Jack, it is Jayantibhai, and I wish you would go away, Raheem."

"I *am*, Dad, I'm being deported. Wow," said Raheem slipping the comb into his back pocket. He no longer appeared to be angry. He snapped his fingers and said, "We're swinging!" to Sam Fong, who turned away so quickly that he nearly knocked Fakhru down. Fakhru had spotted an American and had crept up behind Fong intending to put his arm around him.

Gupta sat on his cracked, weather-beaten valise, his head in his hands, waiting his turn to have his ticket seen, his possessions weighed. There was a wide space around him occupied only by a small boy playing with a large dead bug; a few Indians eyed Gupta from the safety of the crowd, tilted their heads and clucked. Fakhru took Sam Fong by the arm and backed toward Gupta, all the while pointing at the ceiling— distracting the policemen—as he dragged Sam Fong backward. Soon Gupta was directly behind Fakhru.

"Friend Gupta, how goes it?" asked Fakhru.

"This is a sad day for me, an old man leaving for a strange country," sighed Gupta. "But it is also a happy day, for I feel that by leaving I am also serving."

"There is no money in India," said Fakhru.

Gupta ignored the remark. "The Lord Krishna says that the

river never stops and that we must never be at rest. Perhaps now you will see that there is a greater need than ever for us to educate and love the African who has given up part of his homeland that we may prosper..."

"We?" asked Fakhru sharply. His back was still to Gupta; he spoke smiling to the crowd across the lobby.

"We are one people," said Gupta. "All men are broth—"

"Businessmen," said Fakhru. "Except you, Gupta my friend."

"You are very narrow-minded," said Gupta. "Though I am sorry for this unkindness."

"Soon you will be in India or elsewhere," said Fakhru. "Since you have already abused me, then I do not mind saying: *Soon you will be very hungry.* That's what you get for hugging the blacks."

"My mistake is the mistake of us all. I did not love them enough. The *Gita* says ..."

Fakhru walked away dragging Fong with him. "That man is a bloody fool," he said. "I'll bet he cannot even count to a hundred." He stopped ranting about Gupta when he spotted Mehboob wedged between two policemen and a customs official. The customs official was explaining that Mehboob was sixty shillings over the allowed limit. Mehboob was pretending not to understand and asked the African official if perhaps he could explain the snag in Persian.

Two hundred Indians, all relatives of Mehboob, kept their distance. A little courage, thought Fakhru, and I will be nawab. He moved closer to Mehboob, pushing Fong ahead of him; when he spoke he did so without moving his lips, and the policemen would think it was Fong who was speaking. He pressed Fong close to Mehboob and spoke.

"Little trouble?"

"Blacks" was all Mehboob said.

"And Mehboob Paint Supply? Paint, I know I do not have to remind you, dries up very rapidly when it sits idle on shelves."

"You will not let it dry up."

"I am a very busy man," said Fakhru.

"The store, the paint, many good English paintbrushes, some good quality sungoggles, ladders, few all-purpose display cases—the whole *shauri* for four thousand."

"Shillings?"

"Pounds," said Mehboob.

"I can pay you in dollars."

"Where?"

"Karachi, Calcutta, Delhi, you name it."

"It's a deal, then?"

"Three thousand five hundred in dollars, five hundred more in rupees."

Mehboob turned away, looked into the face of the customs official and made his calculations by drumming his fingers quickly on the ticket counter. "That is twenty-five thousand shillings or one thousand two hundred and fifty pounds. I asked four thousand. I will stick to my price, thank you."

"Karachi is a long way from your paint store, brother."

"Fifteen hundred," said Mehboob.

"All right, but only half in dollars. The rest in rupees—and I might throw in a few escudos. You never can tell when you might be in Portugal."

"I am giving it to you free," said Mehboob. "We are being drummed out by these blacks."

The policemen stood closer to Mehboob, confused by the mumbling, the drone that seemed to be coming from Mehboob's direction. But Mehboob, like Fakhru, had not moved his lips. The customs official repeated in Swahili, English and in sign language with impatient gestures that Mehboob would have to surrender sixty shillings.

"Sixty shillings!" shouted Mehboob. "Would you deprive a poor man of sixty bob?" To Fakhru he said, "You're robbing me, but what can I do? I am in no position to argue. *Acha*, thirty thousand, half in dollars, some rupees, and as many escudos as you can manage. Thirty thousand." Mehboob said the numbers slowly, sadly, in Hindi.

"You will get your money in a week, in the land of our fathers. Allah be praised."

J. H. Patel paid his overweight charges and glanced across

the lobby at his relatives, none of whom stood near enough to exchange a word. They fidgeted; most did not look. An old woman wept.

Fakhru edged over, with Sam Fong, toward Patel.

"This is the end of your coffee growing, one would presume," said Fakhru.

"There are my sons," said J. H. Patel. "They will see me through this hardship."

"Are they seeing you through now?" said Fakhru gently. "They are afraid even to whisper to you. Look at them standing there, frightened as mice. Oh yes, they are good people, but will they fetch good prices—will they dare market this year's crop? They will think of what happened to you and hide under their beds. Of course, I don't blame them. But I will feel sorry for you, in Bombay, perhaps living in a doorway, licking the raindrops off motorcars and chewing on rags for nourishment. You cannot make chapaties out of dirt, I will assure you . . ."

J. H. Patel looked at his relatives, all silent except for the wailing granny, bunched together, their dark eyes expressionless, helpless, uncomprehending, twenty feet away.

"The blacks will nationalize your coffee and let the berries rot on the ground."

"I'll sell you half," said Patel, still looking at his relatives.

"How many acres?"

"Six hundred at five hundred pounds an acre. That is pounds sterling."

"Give me eight hundred at four hundred and twenty-five."

"Seven fifty at four forty."

"All right. I know I'm being swindled but I try to help people out of trouble," said Fakhru. "And your pickers. Sign them over."

"You can have two thousand. They are very healthy, as you know."

"I know they had a strike last year. Give me three," said Fakhru looking away.

Patel's eyes were on his silent relatives. "I will not argue; my plane is leaving. Listen carefully. I want to be paid four hundred shillings a man, in Geneva, in German marks. Is that clear? I do not want rupees. This will be confirmed through my brother, S. R. You know him? Good. I will send him a letter of agreement. You will have to see him . . ."

Patel was handed his boarding pass.

> *"Yesssss, it's witchcraft*
> *—ca-razy witchcraft,*
> *And although I know*
> *—It's strictly taboooooooooo."*

"Dino" Raheem was snapping his fingers and doing a little bobbing and weaving dance for the tearful relatives, the wives and children of the deportees. In the empty space between the deportees at the ticket counter and the relatives, a space created by caution and fear, Raheem had ample room to dance.

Patel muttered and said that Raheem was a foolish Moslem. Fakhru heard the remark, but said nothing; he preferred not to ruin a good business deal with petty religious differences. And when Patel repeated the remark, this time rather loudly, Fakhru said, "Indeed. Quite right," in English.

"Look what I've done here! I give credit to the blacks and lose two *dukas*, gifts for charity, coffee for the Five-Year Plan, donations to the Party, the use of my trucks for the singing market mammies—and *this* is what I get for it!" Patel held out his boarding pass, the cardboard crumpled in his brown fist.

"Blecks," said Fakhru hoarsely, calculating the annual coffee yield set against seven hundred and fifty times four forty plus three thousand times twenty, in German marks, at the present rate of exchange . . .

"These blacks," said Patel. "They turn us upside down and shake the money out of our pockets. Then they tell us to go away . . .

"What's that again?" asked Fakhru.

"I said these bloody blacks they turn us upside down, shake out our money, then throw us out."

"I will see your brother, S. R., later," said Fakhru rapidly. "You will like Geneva—His Highness has a home there and speaks very highly of it, and you know what the Lord Krishna says." Fakhru hustled Fong to the front door of the lobby; he told Fong to find his three bodyguards and tell them to meet him immediately at the side of the Main Building, near the runway.

Two planes stood on the runway, an Air India jet and an East African Airways super VC-10. Facing these planes, on the upper viewing deck, stood five thousand silent Asians. On the runway were the police band, ten ranks of Black Guards, some soldiers, the singing market women and what was left of the cabinet. The Prime Minister was just leaving the lounge.

In silence, four figures (one tap-dancing) made their way across the blazing tar of the runway. When they reached the metal stairs of the Air India plane three of the men turned and waved, one bowed and blew kisses with both hands. The crowd of five thousand, composed entirely of brown faces, was impassive, several handkerchiefs appeared from the midst of the faces and then, just as quickly, disappeared. It was as if the five thousand had come to the airport for some other purpose—the sun perhaps—and, caught by surprise, saw some vague acquaintances leaving, whom they dutifully, tolerantly watched, almost sullen in this obligation, since only the fact that it was unexpected and obligatory—not racial or political, but simply social—gave it any importance.

When the jet engines revved up on the Air India plane, the Asians on the upper viewing deck began speaking in a babble of voices that could not be heard above the roar. And after the plane sped down the runway and was in the sky, a renewed silence fell upon the Asians. The eyes of the Asian crowd returned to the runway where the following spectacle was taking place.

Fakhru was being carried, slung by his wrists and ankles like the carcass of a goat, toward the Prime Minister; Fakhru's three Nubian bodyguards did the carrying. Fakhru's face was turned up and his feet, soles to the sky, were on the shoulders of the Nubians.

The Prime Minister stood on a red carpet which led across the runway to the plane. One of his soldiers leaned forward and whispered to him; the Prime Minister shook his head.

Fakhru was brought before the Prime Minister. For a moment he was held, and then he was ceremoniously placed at the feet of the Prime Minister. The soldiers standing near bent closer and cocked their rifles. Fakhru rolled over on the rug, like a hound, and touched his forehead to the glossy shoes of the Prime Minister.

From the upper viewing deck a heavy stillness was breathed forth; all eyes were upon the figure of Hassanali Fakhru, face down, prone on the carpet, in his familiar white pajamas.

Either sensing what was about to happen or else out of exasperation, the Prime Minister swished his fly whisk at Fakhru's head. Fakhru's buttocks rose up, then his shoulders, until he was on his hands and knees. He paused this way for several seconds; then slowly his whole body inched backward along the carpet. When he was about ten feet away he raised his eyes to the Prime Minister. At this gesture, the three Nubians came over, seized his legs and held him upside down.

It was a quick motion. In a matter of seconds Fakhru was hanging vertically in the air before the Prime Minister, bobbing up and down, his clothes and arms flapping loosely; and from his pockets fell two-shilling pieces, half crowns, enormous pennies clanking like doubloons, and tightly wadded notes of every denomination. It went on for a full minute. As soon as the first coins hit the carpet and rolled onto the runway, a cheer went up—first from the ministers, then from the singing market women, then from the Black Guards, then from the soldiers and finally from the five thousand Asians on the upper viewing deck. The police band played the national anthem.

Fakhru was still being shaken, but now nothing fell from his pockets. His arms shot out to the side and he was dropped. The Prime Minister flicked his fly whisk, this time with conviction, briskness; Fakhru grinned broadly, squatted, and bowing toward the Prime Minister's shoes, showed his empty palms. The Nubians seized him again, this time almost roughly, and he was carried off in the direction of the Transit Lounge, as before, like a dead goat.

The Prime Minister raised his arms and received the ovation. His arms dropped; he shouted something and the cabinet ministers fell upon the money which they scooped up and stuffed in a box embossed with the national coat of arms and carried by the Prime Minister's private secretary. Without another word the Prime Minister walked toward the waiting plane, down the carpet, up the silver stairs. On the top step he turned toward the Asians on the upper viewing deck and raised his arms again stiffly as if to say, "You are forgiven." And the deafening cheer which rose from the upper viewing deck was so shrill in its determination that it could have signaled joy or pain.

# 17

SAM FONG HAD WATCHED THE WHOLE SCENE FROM THE UPPER viewing deck by peeping out from behind the sari folds of a very large, curry-scented Indian woman. She was with her family: potbellied husband (Fong was amazed by the size of the man's bare feet which distended his rubber sandals) and three thin-legged boys. While the four Asians walked mournfully across the runway the woman was dishing food out to her family from a basket which she held tightly. In between furtive waves with small handkerchiefs (which they also used to dab their lips), the family gobbled dripping brown sweets the shape and size of golf balls, brittle wafers and glistening yellow objects composed of knotted tubes of juicy dough. When they had wiped the stickiness from their fingers and mouths they looked in the direction of the Air India plane, wagged their balled-up handkerchiefs and sighed.

At first Fong was not sure whether the man prostrate before the Prime Minister was truly Fakhru or not. But certainly the

Nubians were Fakhru's—the colored bows and the broken sword were unmistakable. It was at the end, when the man squatted and showed his empty palms, a characteristic gesture of Fakhru ("I am a poor man—not having money, I tell you") that Fong was sure. That was all Fong saw; he never saw the Prime Minister raise his arms, for just after the money fell the Indian family started on vegetables, and the activity that accompanied this blocked Fong's view.

But he heard the cheers. Staring up at the large Indian man and woman he was impressed by how loudly they could cheer with their mouths filled with cabbage. As the cheer went up, once, twice, from all the Asians around him, Fong felt as if something had just come to an end. It was a definite signal, a deep sigh meaning things would now be different, perhaps better, the Black King appeased by Fakhru kneeling before him; perhaps he would now be able to open his shop. It was an expression of enormous emotion, but still he could not decide if it meant something good or bad was happening. For a clue Fong searched the Asian faces as they cheered, but this did no good because the Asians appeared able to cheer without smiling; they merely opened their mouths and yelled, and the more they yelled the more vacant their eyes became. Gloom seemed to descend as soon as the cheering stopped. Were they happy? Was there a reason for his feeling that something significant had happened, caused by Fakhru and evident in the long silence in which they munched sweets or the deafening cheers in which whole gobbets of the portable dinners were spat onto the runway? Fong could not tell. As the Asians filed out their faces were expressionless, some masked and made inscrutable by heavy eye-narrowing jowls, others shrunken, lined long ago with permanent wrinkles of pain or grief. They all adjusted their clothes, plucked damp cloth away from sticky flesh, fanned themselves and walked with their feet apart, saying *he-hi-hee-chay-ha-hay-hee* without pause and without emphasis.

Fong found Fakhru outside, giggling in the van. They drove home in almost complete silence. What happened on the runway was not mentioned. The only reference was a brief

one, very oblique, by Fakhru: "These *blacks*! These *wahindi*!"
And then laughter and a genial shaking of the head. Just before they turned at the clock tower onto Uhuru Avenue,
Fakhru said, "*And these Americans!*—May I be blessed with a
long life . . ."


The grocery store did reopen. There did seem to be fewer
(and, for some reason, smaller) soldiers on the street. The
Asians did seem to be, at least for a time, off the hook. And
Sam Fong was reasonably happy.

Most of all he was happy because the shop was open; that
meant the canned milk could be sold. Fong did not have business schemes or an income outside the grocery store. He had
passed from the hold of a Chinese freighter to the inside of a
carpentry shop, and from there to the grocery store, without
once intentionally standing in the sun or looking at the huts or
walking in the jungle which sprouted only fifty yards from his
store. That there were possibilities for income outside his store
was irrelevant because of the danger implied in walking into
the unknown. For Fong anything outside his store, the territory beyond the shelves, was spooky, dangerous, murderous.
It did not frighten him because he knew he would never have
dealings beyond the walls of his store. For a long while now,
the shelves, the counters, the empty bins, the mountain of
canned milk crates were as much a part of Fong's household
—his whole world—as the children's low wooden beds or
Soo's shiny-seated stool. Now the boards off the front windows allowed sunlight to enter his store, his life; the mildew
and cobwebs that had accumulated during the State of Emergency were swept away. Some cans of milk were put on the
shelves and their crates made into chairs. Fong believed that
he would have a chance to control his life, to repay his debt
and not have to suffer the humiliation of Fakhru's commands
("Smile." "I am your slave." A painful smile), for as low as
he felt Fakhru's canned milk counter-swindle to have been, he
knew it could only be reversed by a suspension of milk de-
liveries. He maintained his belief in—and even prayed

for—the milk train's imminent derailment, followed by a mob
of white women at his store demanding the cans of milk and
paying high prices.

On the day the grocery store reopened most of the shelves
were filled with cans of milk, many of the bins and vats were
filled and even the large counter had a pyramid of cans on it.
The skin lightener, hair straightener, blood-purifying lozenges, muscle tonic, fat, tea, matches, soap, rice, onions,
cigarettes, Chinese magazines and plastic wallets were
squeezed onto one small shelf. And so they had to be, for no
longer did the sign in front read FRIEND FROCERY POP IN
PLEASE FOR BETTER PRICE ANYWHERE IN AFRICA. The new sign
read SAM FONG FRIEND MILK STORE FOR ALL YOUR MILK
NEEDS. Soo had done this herself, her tongue protruding in
concentration, while Fong and the children stacked the shelves
with the cans of milk.

There were memories: the paint and brush from Mehboob,
the terrifying scene with Mehboob accusing Soo of having
cheated him and now Mehboob elsewhere; the State of Emergency almost at an end, no more nocturnal patterings of feet
and gunshots; like an old brown snapshot, cracked and frayed,
the memory of the small deathly noises at night, during the
first days of the emergency, the family sealed in the store,
eating locusts and listening; the milk swindle that backfired.

Sadly, the memory of the milk—the reminders covering
most of the shelves in the store—ended all reverie and
brought Fong around to the cold thought that 370 shillings
were still owed to Fakhru. Until this was paid Fakhru was at
liberty to tell him to smile, nod or follow him. Even a small
weakness enslaves: Fong chewed on his own proverb and
stared into the stillness of the store.

The milk was on the shelves, most of it, some was still in
the crates; the sign was up, the floor swept; there was nothing
more that could be done. He could not drag the white women
off the street; he could not—as Fakhru had once tried to do—
pay someone to derail the milk train. All that he could do was
all he had ever done since he became the owner of the grocery
store: wait. He wanted to do more, but it was not possible; he

had learned that the *dukawallah* keeps his elbows on the counter and his eye on the door. He smiles. He tries not to eat his stock or, once it is arranged in stacks, interfere in any way with the merchandise. For him, being present is a skill. He stands guard over his stock and waits for money to drop into his biscuit tin so that he can pay his debts and die in peace.

But his debt remained unpaid. The thought of it made Fong's stomach sour and heavy. Fakhru did not threaten him with imprisonment, though once in a while he reminded him of the debt in an offhand way: "I tell you this government owes *millions*—you owe me shillings three seventy only—but this bleck government owes *millions* and I am quite certain . . ." Fakhru had not asked any more favors of Fong. The store was open. The shelves were almost filled. Sunlight splashed through the front window. Everything was fine except that Fong was not making any money.

Fakhru's recent gentle attitude toward Fong developed from the thought Fakhru had that his Chinese friend, so earnestly desired by the Americans, could die of starvation without a murmur, and leave Fakhru stranded. Fong was that sort of fool, a silent and inactive Gupta, seeing nothing, caring about the wrong things, with no sense of values. Several times when Fakhru had this vision of Fong dying without sufficient advance notification he ran to the store and peeked in: each time the Chinaman was leaning on the counter, saying his rosary and smiling into thin air.

Something had to be done to make sure that Fong did not die. Fakhru proposed a plan: Sam Fong would be the agent of Fakhru Enterprises Ltd. The cans of milk took up most of the available space in the store. It was not possible to stock anything else worthwhile—there was no room for it. But Fong could take "orders" for other things and there could be a weekly retainer for this service, plus a commission for anything Fong might sell. Soo was brought into the discussion and together the Chinese couple tried to think of loopholes in the agreement. There did not seem to be any, but that did not mean that there were not any; in a way it meant that there were many large ones. But both Soo and Sam Fong knew,

with what approached horror, exactly what had been sold
since SAM FONG FRIEND MILK STORE opened: two razor blades,
an onion, eleven cigarettes (four filtered, seven plain-tipped
—the plain-tipped were a penny cheaper) and one box of
matches. Two weeks' sales. The milk train showed no signs
of derailment. There was not enough money coming in to stay
alive on; a fresh crop of locusts would not appear until the
rainy season began, and that was months away.

Fong agreed to be Fakhru's agent, and as he agreed, signed
the paper, shook hands, uttered a proverb and listened to
Fakhru saying, "You're doing us both a big favor, friend
Fong. I am believing that you will get rich in this way, as
Christ is my witness . . . ," he felt sure that he was being swindled. He would accept the swindle. But he would get his
weekly shillings and would be able to buy rice and bean seeds
and would know exactly how much he owed, to the penny.
That he would pay when his lotus bloomed or, rather (Fong
quickly corrected the image), when his milk train was derailed.

"These are the American goods for which we negotiated
some time ago," said Fakhru, handing Fong a handbill on
which were listed about fifty items. "You take no-risk-free-
trial basis and sell when you can. I am very busy with my new
coffee *shamba*, paint store and whatnot." Fakhru promised a
weekly retainer of ten shillings, the subsistence allowance,
plus five hundred free handbills which read as follows:

SAM FONG FRIEND MILK STORE
Agents for Fakhru Enterprises Ltd.
Plot 34/DP/67//Z
Uhuru Ave.

Dear Sir/Madam,
    May we introduce ourselves as one of the leading
Grocer, and stocklist of AMERICAN Household & Kitchenware. We are advised to approach you for business relations.
    Our Prices are competitive and we accept Bulk Orders
& Party orders on sale or return basis. We shall be very

oblige if the Reader would humbly give us a chance to serve your Needs, and also please ask you friend & Neighbor to take advantage of us.

We are pleased to inform you the arrival of the following goods *first class*: Buckets & Basins, Pedal dustbin, Lavatory brush & holders, Bread Box, Fridge box, cup, saucer, Schoolchildren, Bottles and Sandwiches Box, Petrol cans, cutlery Trays, Cake and Flour containers, glasses wine, glasses beer, mugs, jags, crokery, teasets, Cup, Fire King Cessaroles, SanckSets Handy.

And also Spoon, Knife fork frypan saucepan broom Brushes & Water Filters, Pressure Lamp, Torch Batteries, Torches, Glasscloths, dishcloths, floor, yellow dusters etc etc, and many more Articles for your Family and Fried.

We are pleased to accept your Requirement. Your visit to our shop saves time and Trouble for Your Daily "Needs." Visit to shop will be Highly Appreciated & most Earnestly Desired by,

> Yours faithfully,
> S. Fong, Mgr.
> *for Hassanali Fukhru Ent. Ltd.*

Soo translated what she could of it for Fong. Fong said, "What about milk?"

"No milk here," said Soo.

"Write milk," said Fong.

Across the bottom of each handbill, in blue pencil, Soo wrote *Milk*.

The handbills were given to Margerine who, instead of slipping them under the doors of white households as he had been directed, brought them to a nearby slum where to his relief all five hundred were eagerly taken by an Arab butcher who promised to distribute them to his customers. He did this by wrapping flyblown joints of goat meat in them.

Fong expected hundreds of white women to respond. He was ready for them: he put his rosary away and watched the door. Each time a white woman drove by (none walked) Fong assured himself that she was looking for a place to park. But the only white woman that entered the store went away empty-handed; she had said what she wanted (to Fong it sounded like "*Nyagah, nyagah*"), and when Fong said, "American goods? Milk?" and held a can in each hand, the woman became angry and shouted, "*No, Nyagah!*" "Nice milk. Good nice milk. Too good nice milk," Fong said. He was still saying it with repetitions and variations as the woman, sighing, walked out of the store.

Three weeks after the handbills were distributed Fong had sold none of Fakhru's goods and none of the milk. He was now certain that Fakhru had swindled him with the American merchandise and the talk about getting rich. The tiny doubt had been dispelled. Fakhru was a crook. Fong wondered why there had been any doubt at all about Fakhru's intentions. Fong had received thirty shillings and had spent it on food. He knew he now owed four hundred shillings. He knew the milk deal was a swindle, the handbills another fraud. But his faith in the train did not waver. He knew it would crash one day; he knew the white women would come. So sure was he of this that he refused to sell any of the milk to Africans. Margerine had asked for, but was refused, a can. Another week passed, another ten shillings from Fakhru, no business and still the feeling that very soon something good was about to happen. Fong braced himself against the counter; he prepared himself for the onslaught of white wives, like the stranger who pauses in a forest and knows very well that there are savage animals and deep holes all around him, but gold and jewels as well; the man who stands silently in the darkness with one hand over his groin and the other hand outstretched waiting for it to touch gold or be bitten off. It was that kind of risk. And one day there was a noise at the door, the sound of clothes, the scuffle of shoes; Fong looked up sharply to see, not the big-nosed face of a white woman at the head of a charge of house-wives, but instead a thin yellow one, almost familiar, unsmiling, and saying, "You are a running dog."

# 18

THE TALK ABOUT ASIAN BLOODSUCKERS AND LEECHES HAD ceased with the Prime Minister raising his arms to the Asians on the upper viewing deck at the airport. Now the Asian community was largely ignored. Where before there had been insult, now there was nothing. Before the Asians had suffered persecution, now they were suffering nothingness, some more than others, but all felt it, for the suffering was actual. The inattention, the nothingness, the neglect hurt them deeply.

S. R. Patel expressed it to Fakhru by saying, "At least before we knew where we stood. They called us bloodsuckers. We called them baboons. They raped up Sheth's daughter. We gave them few kicks. Gupta waves his arms and says, 'Help the poor blacks.' We say no. We make a little money on the black market. They chisel us out of Party donations and free credit. We swindle them. They break our windows. A fair fight—everybody knows what the sides are, everybody knows what's going on. Now," he sighed, "they deported J. H.

and the rest of them. You make a big *shauri* at the airport. Nobody calls anybody bloodsucker. Nobody says nothing. Nobody even gets deported again, no broken windows, no more kicking houseboys. Business as usual. Nobody knows what's going to happen next. I'm bloody sick of it, man."

Fakhru made sure the papers for the coffee *shamba* were in order. He had the signatures of V. B., M. K. and R. H. Patel as witnesses. He sipped his tea and sampled some *laddhu* and then, swallowing, he shook his head and spoke.

"That's a nice speech and some of it is true. But don't you see," he said, "they are still baboons?"

"How are we supposed to know that?" asked S. R. dejectedly. "They don't call us leeches."

"We were never leeches!" said Fakhru sharply, grinning. "They were always baboons."

To prove his point, Fakhru told S. R. a story. A sahib up-country was on his veranda drinking one afternoon; it was a lovely day and the man was lucky enough to have a large mango tree in the garden. "What nice chutney I could make from those mangoes," the sahib said. He went over to the tree and peered up into the branches. He was astonished to see his houseboy curled up and dozing on a branch, his arms hanging down, his cheek against the bark of the branch. "Hello there! What are you doing?" shouted the sahib. "But sah," said the houseboy, "I thought you gave me home leave."

"So you see," said Fakhru, "there's nothing to worry about. They are the same."

"Fakhru*bhai*, I tell you it would make me very happy if they were out on the street there throwing big stones through my windows! I like things to be normal: they throw stones through my windows; you ask me who is doing such a dreadful thing; I say *blacks*! Who are you? you ask. I am S. R. Patel, I reply. Hah! Such a thing is not possible now."

S. R. was getting excited. When he described the Africans throwing stones through his windows he had a crooked smile on his face; his voice was louder than was necessary, shrill, and it cracked as he grinned and gulped through his description of the African rock-throwers. Fakhru looked concerned;

he did not consider S. R.'s reaction to be a healthy one.

"You have a little *duka*, don't you?" Fakhru began.

"Little *duka*, a medium-size, yes."

"You selling a little housewares, few dry goods, so forth?"

"Indeed. And the coffee *shamba* . . ."

"You make a little . . ." Fakhru pursed his lips and looked down; he pretended to be counting money by a rapid motion of his fingertips.

"Little bit," said S. R.

"So what you worrying about?" said Fakhru in irritation.

"I worrying about . . ." S. R. did not finish the sentence; it was as if he could not think of what was worrying him, although Fakhru gave him time to think and did not interrupt. Several full minutes passed; S. R.'s mouth was open, but he did not speak. Still he looked very worried.

"Africa," Fakhru said, breaking the silence (he hoped to bring S. R. around; S. R. looked as if he had just been kicked out of the world), "—it's no place to raise kids. Of course, I have my own solution. If the blecks get in my way I just *kick*—" Fakhru kicked some sawdust on S. R.'s floor. "That way they respect you. They like big *bwanas*—they don't like some little chap weeping and crying. You must be firm and tough with them. *Hoot* at them! Even strike them, my friend. Just yesterday I had to . . ."

S. R. turned his eyes upon Fakhru; they were veined red like bad yolks, like the eyes of a religious fanatic. His lower lip trembled; it was perfectly dry. "I can't sleep," said S. R. "I'm not ashamed. This is true. I don't know what is going to happen to me. I can't take food, maybe little bit *dal*, few rice. I *worry*, I *suffer*. I say to my wife, 'Let's we go to Canada. Ramesh is in Canada—we have nice time, no worry.' She asked me is Canada near Abyssinia. I can't explain it. Where is the world? I feel like a radio—nice clean Japanese-type, shiny good batteries . . . but . . ." S. R. looked down and groaned, "*But no programs*. No programs, nothing but wires inside me, no programs, no talking in here, you see what I mean?"

"You suffering, isn't it?"

"Too much," said. S. R. He breathed a sob.

"My advice to you is, *Go to Canada*. And if you're look-ing for a buyer for your little *duka*, household wares, so forth, you can count on me. I gave J. H. a fair price for his coffee. I do the same for you . . ."

"Publicity American-style!" said Fakhru foolishly, handing Mel Francey ten of Fong's handbills for inspection. Mel fin-gered one of them, wrinkled up his face and looked at Fakhru.

"Sam Fong Friend Milk Store," he grunted. "What the hell kinda store is *that*?"

"Milk store. Like shoe store, cycle store, vegetable store. *Duka* for selling milk in," he explained.

"Any money in milk hereabouts?"

Fakhru said it wasn't the milk, it was the agency for Amer-ican goods that would bring Fong a profit. "He sells milk, yes—but he takes orders for all sorts of things you see listed on that chit. He will be doing very well. He might even get—*rich!*" Fakhru giggled. He hated himself. He knew he was behaving like an ass. Talking to Americans always threw him off-balance; he could not prevent himself from acting foolish or talking too much. From this provocation to foolishness which he felt when he faced most Europeans or Americans, came his contempt for these people, shared by nearly his whole community. What sometimes made it worse was when he remembered Gupta's warning: "In the eyes of the white man you are as black as these Africans and more dangerous."

Fakhru was still talking about Fong ("You have nothing to worry about; I will keep him well stocked with American goods, ha-ha"), but Mel was not listening. He stared at the badly printed, misspelled handbill of unbleached newsprint paper and shook his head. These mothers have a long way to go, he thought. Such thoughts crossed his mind only when he was confronted by definite evidence of the simplicity and smallness of the lives and ambitions in East Africa. At other times (he might be showing someone how to thread a film projector or stack pamphlets) the hopelessness of the whole place would leave him and he would laugh, sometimes too loudly, and think: I'm getting twenty grand a year for this! (He once said this to a stranger in a nightclub in Addis Ababa as they watched a very thin Negress remove her clothes to the *pong* of a wooden xylophone.) In the same way the hopelessness of the Fong scheme left him. He took another look at the handbill and laughed.

"Yes?" asked Fakhru, tilting his head.

"Supposin—just supposin we send someone in that there milk store to buy somethin, spend a little money, know what I mean?"

"You mean tell someone to go to the milk store and buy goods?" Fakhru looked puzzled.

"Well, I'm just spit-ballin—this ain't no *idea* or anythin like *that*!" Mel laughed. "I jess thought this'd be a hell of a lot simpler if we sent a couple of people in there to juice up the whole operation, spearhead it, so to speak. What do you think of that?"

Fakhru stared at Mel. He said nothing.

Mel continued. "I mean we pay some people to go in there and buy from the Chinaman. Simple as pie."

"Pay someone? To buy?" Fakhru twitched.

"Yeah. That's it." Mel bobbed his head and said "Yeah" again. He was thinking of his salary and smiling.

Fakhru shaped his lips. At first no sound came out, but soon there was a noise, a dry one, something like, *"Vhai?"*

"What's that?"

Fakhru tried very hard. *"Vhai* are you saying this?"

"Whah?"

"Yesss, please."

"'Cause we think it's a good idea, that's whah!" said Mel, wondering if it was a good idea. "Anyway, it wouldn't do no harm now, would it?"

"No," said Fakhru. "No harm, certainly." Good heavens, thought Fakhru, and turned gray.

"So what's the objection?"

Fakhru's face stayed gray. "It might be dear," he finally said.

*"Dear?"*

"Costive. It might be costive, isn't it?"

"So what?" Mel stared at Fakhru, as if Fakhru had said "It might be blue" to someone who was color-blind.

"Needless . . . expense, maybe no profit, just . . . throwing money . . . As we say, business is busin . . ."

"Shit, man, you can't measure good will in dollars and cents! What kinda cheap bastards you think we Americans are? Sure, I agree, bidnis is bidnis, but *this here* ain't bidnis! This here's good will, *frinship!*" Mel set his face close to Fakhru's and said, "Besides, you yourself said it won't do no harm and, brother, if it don't do no harm what difference does it make *how* much it gonna cost?"

Fakhru wanted to say, If you Americans were not so rich I would say you are crazy and quite dangerous, but good manners prevented him. He said simply, "Indeed," and let it go at that.

Mel sensed Fakhru's bewilderment. But the more awed and bewildered Fakhru became, the more convinced Mel was that he was doing the right thing, that his plan could not miss. Briefly, it would require making Fong rich without actually handing him the money. He would discover fun, broads, greed, throwing money around, putting people to work, all the bonuses of capitalism, the corruption of comfort and so forth. Mel told Fakhru how a man becomes a Communist: just like a drowning man he will grab anything. He told Fakhru about Communists he had known, about their crummy teeth, rotten health, awful clothes, Barney Oldfield caps, joyless lives. The object was to make Fong happy, content, preferably rich, and with a strong suspicion that America made him that way. After that he would be useful in telling the world the truth about Communism. He said that Fong had proved to be a tough nut to crack.

"When he is cracked you will be heppy?"

"Not me necessarily," said Mel. "But the world'll be a better place, know what I mean?"

"No."

"Take Africa. You take your average underdeveloped African country and average gutfull of growing pains. Then you stick in a Chi-com and, brother, you've got trouble, don't think you haven't."

"I am not understanding."

"What *are* you, a Communist? Here I am explaining the whole thing to you. The trouble with you, Fakra, is you jess don't *wanna* understand, that's all. You want me to spell it out for you ABC? *Jesus*." Mel rolled his head.

"You mean this fellow Fong? You think he's annoying the blecks?"

"Annoying? No *sir*. Killin, screwin up, burnin, *yes*! I tell you, he's—" Mel leaned closer to Fakhru "—he's the one that's responsible for this here emergency thing, sure as shootin. Why you think the Old Man's so het up for?"

Fakhru tittered.

"You laffin? I tell you we *know* that guy's messin around. We got him watched, don't ask me by who. We know everyone that's messin around here."

"The blecks, no?"

"No. The yallers."

"Fong?"

"Right. Fong. That's our man."

Fakhru sighed. "Let me just say I have lived almost my whole life here in East Africa. My father traded in cashews on the coast. I know the blecks. If there is trouble here, it is the blecks. The trouble is never serious because the blecks cannot do very much. They are as lazy in breaking down as they are in building up. You see, there was what they called emergency here where any poor fellow could be arrested *kabisa* for no reason at all. That simple chap Fong had nothing to do with that—it was the blecks, I know them very well indeed..." Fakhru continued to explain, first using his experience and talking about the deportations; he told how, using a simple trick at the airport, he had single-handedly convinced all the politicians, and especially the Old Man, that the Asians "were good cheps." He acted out his airport trick and showed how the money had dropped out of his pockets. Mel did not seem convinced. Fakhru told his jokes, the one about the sahib's houseboy and another about the banks' taking on African members of staff and making them "branch managers." Finally he said, "You have not been here very long. You will see. Yes, it is true, all men are brothers—but the blecks are our younger brothers. You do not fully understand the blecks . . ."

While Fakhru was speaking Mel had risen out of his chair. He was now facing Fakhru.

"Now don't tell me the so-called blacks did *that*!" said Mel.

"I am telling you, sir. The blecks run this country. They make the laws. They raped Sheth's daughter. They break our shopwindows and deport us. The blecks want to kill us all. If they had more arrows they would do it."

"No, they *wouldn't*!"

"How do you know, if you please?" Fakhru said saucily.

"Cause *I'm* black and *I know*."

Fakhru did not speak. He simply folded his hands and took a good look at Mel. He knew something was going wrong.

"Now *back up*!" Mel said loudly. "For your information, buddy-boy, *I'm a black*! You see that skin?" He held his huge forearm in Fakhru's face. "That's *black* skin."

"No, it's not," said Fakhru in polite correction. "It's brown, like . . . like *mine*." He smiled.

"It ain't like yours. It's *black*!"

In this rare moment, when the words of persecution that Mel had always suspected were being whispered were actually spoken, Mel was at one with the Africans. It was "These are my people" once again, and not because he had changed his mind about them (they still pissed in broad daylight against the side of National and Grindlay's), but because of Sam Fong, the menace who was responsible for the emergency, and Hassanali Fakhru, who represented, in his brown contempt, all the insult that Mel had endured, real or imagined; and in this loveless chaos which the impoverished Africans endured it was clear to Mel why the embassy took no notice of Asians. Mel was also very happy. Again he was a person, no longer a perfect stranger. He was scoring.

Fakhru backed up. He continued to look at Mel's arm (Mel was rolling up his sleeve). He thinks he is black, thought Fakhru.

"What you're saying is plain racial prejudice. It's nothing new to me—I'm used to it," Mel said with pain in his voice. "But, Fakra, I thought you and me were frins . . ."

"We *are* friends," said Fakhru. "I had no idea . . ."

"Don't you *see*? I'm an Afro-American."

"You are?"

"You bet," said Mel. "And I can tell you it ain't the Africans screwin up this country. It's the Commies. I tell you, Fong's our man."

Even as much as Fakhru hated Gupta, the Hindu meddler, he could not blame him for the trouble. And the idea that the incompetent Fong could be responsible for the near overthrow of the government when he obviously had problems with his own small *duka*—it was so ridiculous that Fakhru almost laughed. He would have laughed, but he knew that somehow he had offended Mel ("I'm *black*, I tell you!") and so he kept his mouth shut. He let Mel tell him about what the Chinese had done in a dozen countries, making it look as if the Africans could not run their own affairs, buying and selling people left and right like cans in a grocery store. And while Mel spoke, Fakhru, who was after all a business man, put two and two together, thought of Fong and said to himself: So that is why . . .

There was not much more. The conversation hit a definite slump when Mel sided with the Africans, but Fakhru managed to say "Indeed, if we give them a chance . . . multi-racial society . . . build the nation . . . *harambee* . . . let bygones be bygones . . ."

And at the very end Mel explained that they were throwing a party for Fong, a big splash ("We're gonna use psychological warfare on him . . ."). As he said this, explained the party, he sadly realized that only Fakhru could get Fong to the party. And Fakhru himself, of Hassanali Fakhru Enterprises Ltd., had this very thought the moment it crossed Mel's mind. Mel reflected that however honky and big-mouth biased and twoassed about race relations Fakhru was, he was more or less indispensable. While the friendship was certainly at an end, Fakhru would continue to act as a middleman; without sympathy the plot against Fong would continue, and from both points of view—it saddened Mel a great deal to think that since he was now sure he hated Fakhru's guts—business was booming.

# 19

YOU ARE A RUNNING DOG, MR. CHEN HAD SAID. IT WAS THE prologue to a torrent of abuse, all of which Fong bore in silence, the large counter his only protection against Mr. Chen and his partner. First one, then the other harangued him, told him he was a lackey, a leech, a disgrace to China.

Fong said nothing; he had started to object but was silenced by more abuse. The men did not look harmful, though they were certainly impolite. Still, they were Chinese and their accent was good—thirty-five years of speaking Swahili had taken the edge off Fong's. He wondered why they chose him to insult; the insults were odd. *A disgrace to China?* It reminded Fong vaguely of one of his first dealings with Fakhru in which Fakhru accused Fong of "giving Asia a bad name." That remark bemused Fong at the time, and he was further bemused when Mr. Chen said something similar, for China, indeed, all of Asia in his mind, was nothing more than one muddy little hillside paddy with three huts, all leaky, some naked children, his playmates, and two oxen. There was also a bridge which washed away every year, and some wild-flowers. The two Chinese in the shop hissing like snakes rapped against this vision and disturbed Fong's reverie. They said they had seen the Americans in his shop many times, and Indians too, bloodsuckers all of them, weakening the country and causing chaos. Fong had dealings with them, had sold out to them, he was a jackal in Marxist clothing, a puppet, a fascist octopus who would soon sing his swan song because he was pursuing a revisionist line. They knew; they had watched him. They knew every move he made. "You are never out of our sight," said Mr. Chen.

Their harangue had not gone on long. But it was nonstop; one got his breath while the other hissed. At the end they reached into briefcases and withdrew bundles of magazines and clean new books: *The Quotations of Chairman Mao Tse-tung*, with a red washable plastic cover, *China Reconstructs, China Pictorial, Peking Review, The Selected Military Writings of Mao Tse-tung* in a boxed edition with a silk ribbon bookmark sewn to the binding and *The Peoples' Songbook* which, when thrown on Fong's counter, opened unaccountably to "As a Paddy Field is Plowed the Afro-Asians Will Dig Up All the Shackles of Colonialism and Imperialism While Chairman Mao Shines Like a Red Sun in Our Hearts." They screeched again, this time in unison, and said that Sam Fong should carry the revolution to the end, that he should stop being a tool of the Yankee imperialists and that he would see them again.

The Chinese had skulked in and accused. They left the store unseen. Mel Francey arrived in the embassy Chevy with Fakhru, a mob of Africans running alongside the car. No secrecy, no skulking was involved. Secrecy was out of the question; it would not have been psychological warfare. The aim was to make Fong feel wanted.

It was the long, shiny, unblemished car, the two American flags attached to chrome posts on the huge fenders, the license plate USA-32 and also Mel, a large clean man, that drew the hostile crowd. (Everything large and new has the fascination of arrogance in a poor country where things are little, usually dirty and are not seen; or if they are large are invariably in disrepair.) Mel was wearing his straw hat, a light-colored jacket with matching shorts instead of trousers and sandals. The outfit, and the fact that he was sitting in the back seat— the car driven by an old man—made Mel look like a large silly child in his father's car. He got out and walked toward SAM FONG FRIEND MILK STORE FOR ALL YOUR MILK NEEDS. Fakhru followed.

The crowd gathered to stare. The driver snapped insolently at them, but they refused to disperse. Mel smiled, oblivious of the hostility, and shook a few moist hands saying, "*Jambo!* Howsa boy . . . *Jambo!* Howsit goin, buddy-boy!" etc. He was met by reproachful gazes; no one spoke except Mel, and before he came anywhere near the entrance to Fong's *duka* both American flags were pinched from the fenders. The flags, passed from hand to hand, ended up at the doorway where two small boys wagged them in Mel's face.

Mel was delighted. He snapped a picture with his pocket camera and murmured, "Warm welcome in jungle outpost. We are loved everywhere," as if supplying a title.

All Fakhru's anger was roused when he saw large crowds of Africans. He imagined them traveling in mobs, in herds which destroyed—ate, broke, defiled—everything in their path. While Mel grinned and winked at the hostile faces, Fakhru shouted, "Go back to sleep, you bastards! *Toka!* Go away! Can't you see we have big business here? What are you looking at, you bugger! You never saw a white man before? What is the big *baraza* for? Piss off, *wananchi*, back to the trees and stop troubling . . ."

From the crowd came a chorus: "*Muheendi mshenzi!* . . . Indiani stupeedi . . . Bloody Indiani . . . *kondo!* . . . Lobber! . . . Blood sheet . . . You beeg sheet *kabisa!* . . ."

Mel smiled and continued waving.

Fong saw them coming. He was in the same position when, ten minutes previously, Mr. Chen and the small fellow had harangued him. The pile of magazines lay on the counter, the *Peoples' Songbook* still open to the song about the Afro-Asian digging up colonial shackles.

Trained in such things, Mel was able to greet Fong warmly and mentally note the name of every pamphlet and book on the counter as soon as he entered the store. He was not surprised to see them there; he had read every one of them. The fact that they were in English did not trouble him in the least. The presence of the *Military Writings* confirmed what he had said about Fong; he reminded himself to tell Fakhru about it, Fakhru who had said, "If there is trouble in this country, it is the blecks."

"Buying nice milk?" Fong said to Mel. When he saw Fakhru his face fell and he said, "*Selling* nice milk?"

"We're not here to sell you a thing," said Mel, taking out a large square envelope with an eagle embossed in gold on the flap. This he placed on top of the *Peoples' Songbook*.

Fakhru translated. "In this big-big envelope is a special discount chit, very cheap, you pay me later if you are interested. With this chit you are able to sell milk to all Americans."

Mel looked eagerly at Fong, hoping for a smile.

Fong was confused. "Look around. Look at all the goods. No money, just goods." He gestured at the crates of milk, the cans on the shelf.

"The Americans are having a big *baraza*—buying and selling as well—at the big-big fancy embassy house. You can sell many cans there."

"They want milk?"

"These people want everything. But to enter their *duka* you need this chit. *Bwana* here is asking do you want to buy."

"How much for the chit?"

"Not much. Little-little. Hundred only. You don't have to pay me with real money. Say yes, finish. You owe me just the same. Take the chit and then you owe me an even five hundred."

Fong looked at the envelope. It was pure white; the eagle gleamed on it. He picked it up.

"Too pretty this chit. Costing more than hundred only," said Fakhru.

"What're you saying?" asked Mel impatiently. And before Fakhru could answer he asked, "What's *he* saying? He wanna come?"

"It appears he wants money, though he is reluctant to accept it here while his family watches. Note an exceeding number of faces in the doorway."

"Tell him to name his price," said Mel, looking around the shop.

Fakhru turned to Fong. "He says he will sell you the chit for shillings seventy-five only, special today. Six months to pay, no *down payment* . . ."

"Yeah," said Mel, hearing Fakhru's only English phrase, "Whatever it is, tell him it's jess a down payment. There's a bundle more to come if he plays along." He looked at Fakhru with pleasure. "You know, Fakra, you sure are a sonofabitch, but you got a helluva good head for bidnis."

Mel felt he had at least zeroed in on Fong; with the help of Fakhru, of course. Another success, a little sunlight let in through the bamboo curtain. It had not been easy, but in a world populated by Chinese saboteurs of Fong's ilk, racists like Fakhru with whom one had to do business both at home and abroad and red tape—Bert's title for the report (or was it *red-handed*? He could not remember, though he knew it was catchy)—what *was* easy?

"I try my best, *bwana*," said Fakhru bowing. "He wants shillings five hundred only."

"Give him six hundred," said Mel with enthusiasm.

"I offer sixty," said Fong.

"He accepts it," said Fakhru in English; and in Swahili, "*Anaikubali*, he accepts it."

# 20

"INVITE ALL YOUR FRIENDS, FAKRA," SAID MEL, "PROVIDING they're Africans."

Fakhru had come to know that Mel was not joking. Using his own invitation as a model, he had his friend Bhimji print several dozen more, and these he hawked shamelessly to Africans around town at fifty shillings apiece. Shoogra did the inscriptions with a thick nibbed pen.

The night of the embassy gala in Fong's honor, Fakhru drove to the *duka* in his gray van. Fong stood in the doorway, his invitation clutched tightly in his hand. Fong was not wearing his cork helmet as he usually did when he went out. He wore an old, pin-striped, gray woolen suit that was creased with a hundred little squares and angles as if it had been folded as small as it would go and then stored squashed under something heavy. His collar tips curled upward, his wide, frayed tie hung outside his oversized jacket; on his feet were soiled tennis shoes which his trouser cuffs covered completely. Shoogra was in a sari of gold brocade; Fakhru wore a clean set of pajamas.

As they drove away Fong looked back. Soo was not sitting on her stool. She was standing behind the counter where, for well over four years, Fong had stood. Her neck was straight; she stared through the door.

The American Ambassador's residence was in the center of town, across from Parliament. Formerly the house of a colonial officer, it had, in addition to a large veranda hung with vines, a private zoo in the back and terraced gardens extending to a post-colonial swimming pool with lights glowing inside it. A slum of grass-roofed shacks lay beyond the embassy fence ("You've got your *very own village!*" a visitor had once remarked to the ambassador). In Fong's honor, paper lanterns —they were Japanese—had been strung along the driveway, across the veranda and even over lights inside the house. A paper dragon and a paper tiger dangled from the ceiling; on the walls were scrolls with oriental writing on them. In plates around the room were fortune cookies, small Buddhas and smoldering joss sticks. It was as if someone had collected a bit of junk in every bazaar from Beirut to Tokyo and brought it all intact to the ambassador's house. For balance, to compensate for the farrago of oriental knickknacks, American flags were everywhere: on a tall pole on the front lawn, over the fireplace, and in every corner of the house. There was a photograph of President Kennedy chatting with the ambassador; under this picture the two statesmen were identified and there was a quotation under their names to the effect that Africa was the last frontier and that the "New World" would accept the challenge of this "Newer World," not because the Communists were doing a lot but because it was the right thing to do. The house was large, the living room alone held four huge sofas and a dozen chairs.

In spite of the many places to sit, when Fong entered with Fakhru and Shoogra everyone was standing, and among these standing people, at the entrance of the three Asians, there was a hush which quickly became a dead silence. The silence lasted a long time, and in fact was not broken by the ambassa-

dor introducing himself to Fong and saying that *his* name was
Sam, too. It was not broken by the ambassador's wife who,
full of charm and speaking idiotically slow, said that she had
deliberately decorated the place *à la mode Chinoise*, as she
put it. It was not broken by Mel's or Bert's glad hand or by the
cautious greeting of first one and then another member of the
embassy staff. And when the ambassador said that he too was
an Indian—at least his mother was, though not an "India Indian" like Fakhru, but rather a "Red Indian," a Comanche to
be exact—the silence seemed heavier, more intense, like the
noiselessness at the airport when all the Asians watched
Fakhru kneeling before the Prime Minister and waited for a
signal, not knowing that the silence itself was a signal. The
silence in the ambassador's residence stopped time and made
people conscious of their breathing, and most of all it made
those in the room conscious of the little yellow man in their
midst, flanked by Fakhru and the ambassador and backed up
by Mel and Bert, like a rare trophy brought back alive from a
jungly distant land everyone knew existed but which no one,
save Mel and Bert, had visited. The little yellow man did not
blink; he may not even have had his eyes open; he stood—the
smallest person in the room—and held tight to the frayed
cuffs of his jacket sleeves. His hair was carefully parted: it
was pure white, for although his face was not lined, he was
old. His certain age occurred to the people watching in silence, but it was his creased woolen suit and not his age that
was as awesome and almost as damning as the fact of his race.

The ambassador's wife stirred again. All eyes followed
her, waiting for relief. She put on a record. "Slow Boat to
China" was followed by "My Little China Doll," songs from
an LP entitled *Slant-Eyed Symphony*. It did little to relieve;
everyone listened in silence to the words and watched Sam
Fong. They were people who were unaccustomed to silence,
who were comforted by the racket of their own voices. Stillness made them nervous and jumpy, aware of the silence they
dared not break, and ashamed of the noiseless fidgeting they
considered unforgivably rude.

It was not until the Africans arrived that things got moving.

The Africans who had bought invitations from Fakhru arrived
first, with clamor, and made for the bar. The embassy person-
nel merrily pounced on them, like old friends, cornered them
in twos and threes, filled their glasses, remarked on their
bright shirts and even on their color ("If I come back to earth a
second time, I want to come back black, just like you," said
one of the embassy men to an African who replied, "Sure,
*bwana*, why not?"). With the arrival of the Africans the once
silent embassy staff succeeded in raising the level of noise to a
comfortable din. Shortly after, other Africans showed up, the
politicians, members of parliament, the chairman of the Lint
Marketing Board, a political scientist, a banker and a dentist.

These last were the regulars. They were invited to all embassy parties and were now thoroughly bored with them—
bored with them to the extent that they made only the
minimum conversation, greeted only the senior embassy offi-
cials and drank without pause. They resented the fact that they
were continually invited to the parties and were unable to
refuse. Now they viewed the invitations as a gross form of
persecution about which they were frankly and quite openly
critical. Out of spite, the regulars made a point of never reci-
procating invitations. They took pride in the fact that an
American had never set foot in their houses. But the American
hostesses repeatedly said that in Africa no party was complete
without at least a few African faces. And so the regulars were
never dropped from the guest list, a kind of slavery they felt
helpless to prevent. The regulars said that they were the most
familiar of all with shackles and chains that enslaved, that
could be felt but not seen, and were stronger than iron. It was
foreign domination all over again.

With the arrival of the Africans Sam Fong moved—or
rather, was pushed—to a corner. Fakhru had not been lying: it
really was a big *baraza*. There were well over a hundred people in the room. A good chance to sell a little milk, buy a few
tires, make a little money and then go home to bed. Fong
allowed a man to get him a drink. That is, he said yes to a
man's incomprehensible question and seconds later found
himself with a tall icy glass. It froze his hand. He looked for a

place to put it down. Seeing a small table near the window he edged over, but as soon as he had placed the glass on the table something moved outside.

Cupping his hands to the sides of his eyes Fong peered out the window. Peering back through the glass, and wearing a seedy suit much like his own, was Mr. Chen, moths settling on his face and other insects strafing him. "Lackey!" yelled Mr. Chen with incautious loudness and then he disappeared.

Fong felt no emotion. Mr. Chen represented only the tiny but very noisy number of troublemakers that began to appear in China shortly before he left. Fong knew they were anti-government and atheistic, that they burned churches and blew up bridges. What Fong wondered was how this Chen fellow had gotten as far as Africa. Perhaps he had been driven out by the Christians. Fong was not disturbed by Chen's shrieking; he had few memories of the Chinese speaking softly to one another. It seemed they always shrieked. He gave Mr. Chen no further thought.

From his place near the window Fong watched the First Secretary towering over Shoogra who sipped at her Coca-Cola. "I been all over the world," said the First Secretary. "Been to Hong Kong, Bangkok, Calcutta, Benares—your neck of the woods, right?—Agra, Delhi. Saw the Taj Mahal by night and then the next day, by day—Karachi, Rome, Athens, London, Shannon. And let me tell you—and India, *Christ*, I don't know *how* she's gonna, no offense, solve her problems sort of, with the high birth rate and all. But as I was saying, let me tell you: *people*, I don't know, *they're all the same*, you know what I mean?"

Shoogra stared. Her Coke had gone flat. She watched the First Secretary drain his glass and then purse his lips.

"Sure," he went on, "it takes a few drinks for people to become their real selves. There was this college professor, a bright little guy in Bangkok—no, Bangalore, I think it was Bangalore—we had a few and he loosened up, cut the sahib crap and he was telling me the same thing: they're all the same, regardless of the color of a man's skin. And you know? I think that's just great."

Shoogra did not react. Not because she was a Moslem and did not like the First Secretary saying, "It takes a few drinks for people to become their real selves," but because her English was faulty and she was not quite sure what he was saying. The First Secretary took her silence to mean disapproval of his sentiments. His tone turned to pleading.

"I know you Indians aren't crazy about Africans. But Jesus, you gotta realize that Africans are just like everyone else, only darker."

Fong went for his glass again. A man was standing near it. Fong approached him and said, *"Unajua kiswahili, bwana?"*

The man grinned and said, with gestures, "Me. No. Speak Chi-nese. Me. Speak. Eng-lish."

"Buying milk?" Fong took his crumpled invitation out of his jacket pocket and showed it to the man.

"Me. No. Speak." The man began again. He raised his arms to gesture, but just as quickly dropped them to his sides and gave up. He walked away, muttering.

Fong picked up his glass and gulped it. He felt his bladder swell and then go taut.

"Africa. Big deal," a voice to Fong's left whined. "Mountains, trees, flowers, coons, unforgettable scenery. Man, I've had it up to here. If you ask me I'd say it's pretty goddamned forgettable. The other day I was saying to my wife, 'Helen, everything you see in Africa—every last thing—you could see five miles out of Washington, D.C.' That's what I said to her and she said, 'Bob, honey, you're dead right.' Africa, big deal!"

"There are nice zoos here," was the rejoinder. The woman who spoke had the hard face of a barfly.

"Zoos! Don't talk to me about zoos! Ever seen the zoo in Damascus? Now *there's* a zoo."

"There's a swell one in Caracas, now that you mention it."

"And did you ever see the one in Kuala Lumpur? Near the what's-its-name?"

"The Esso station?"

"No. The . . . the . . . museum thing."

"No, never saw it."

"That's a shame. I think that one's tops."

"When were you in Borneo?"

"Kuala Lumpur's not in Borneo, for Christ's sake. It's in thing, in Malaya. I was there three years. I'm an old Far East hand. Saigon, too. Boy, *there* was a city. No bananas in Saigon, you can bet your butt on that."

"Saigon? Veetnam?"

"Oh, sure. You could *live* there. It's gone down a lot, though. The fucking Chinese have..." He did not finish the sentence. He apologized, not to the lady with whom he was talking, but to Sam Fong whom he saw eying him.

Fong slipped away, and the man said, "I've really done it now. Just like when I was in Tokyo in forty-six and forgot the war was over."

"You seem to have traveled quite extensively," said the lady.

"In this racket you gotta keep moving," the man said. He walked quickly to the bar where Mel and Bert, surrounded by listeners, told of the difficulties they had in winning over Fong. The party seemed more theirs than Fong's. For once, no one offered information about communists he had known; no one, it seemed, had ever met one. "It was a real bitch," said Mel. "He's tough as nails, that Red," said Bert. "Heartless. He'd sell his mother down the river..."

Fong went to the side door and looked for a toilet. He peeked into several corners, behind some potted ferns and into the hallway; he saw nothing that resembled a toilet, nowhere to relieve himself. He thought of going outside and pissing against the house, but he knew Mr. Chen was there waiting for him. Mr. Chen would corner him and begin yelling. Fong saw Fakhru talking to one of the embassy wives. Fakhru was saying that he had always wanted to visit the States; it was his one dream and someday he would do it. Hearing this an African appeared. He had apparently misheard the conversation; he was under the impression that the woman Fakhru was talking to was interviewing Fakhru for a free trip to the States to go on a study-course. The African asked for a free ticket. When he made this request the woman turned away from

Fakhru, ignored him totally (Fakhru was still speaking as the woman turned) and began talking to the African. Fong made a sign to Fakhru.

Fakhru came over. "How is your milk selling?" he asked.

"No milk selling," said Fong. "I am searching for the *choo*. Where is pissing? I want to piss and then go home."

"Not now. This is your fat chance. You will have a lot of *baraka* here, selling milk. First selling, then pissing." He swung Fong around to the First Secretary and introduced Fong, then himself.

The First Secretary was drunk. He eyed Fong with suspicion and tried to hear what Fakhru was saying (in the center of the room some Africans were demonstrating a native dance; they were hooting and clapping in rhythm).

"Very nice party," said Fakhru. "My esteemed friend Fong enjoys it very much."

The First Secretary looked at Fong. Fong smiled. The First Secretary looked wildly into his glass and then drank.

"Oh, he is very heppy indeed," said Fakhru expectantly.

"Thass what we like to hear," said the First Secretary and he walked away.

"You've just sold three crates. I am authorized to pay you," said Fakhru. He dragged Fong into the hallway and stuffed sixty shillings into Fong's side pocket saying, "You're a lucky fellow selling this milk. You can't go home now."

Fong looked at Fakhru. Beyond Fakhru's beaded cap, in the corner near a large carving, was Mr. Chen, glowering.

"Do you know that *muntu*?" asked Fong.

"Which one?" Fakhru turned, but Mr. Chen had disappeared.

"You have drunk too much *pombe*," said Fakhru.

The ambassador appeared where Mr. Chen had been, as if the wily oriental had changed himself into a paunchy half-breed with big square jowls and a shiny silk suit.

"You were saying," said Fakhru to the ambassador, "your mother was an Indian."

"Sure was," said the ambassador. "And not only mine. Lots of people in this very room—Americans just like you and me"—the ambassador said this automatically, as though everyone he spoke to was an American—"they've got *tons* of Indian blood in them. Mel Francey, you know Mel, claims his granddaddy was a Seminole from Tallahassee. Who'm I to say he's lying!" It was clear from the ambassador's tone, however, that Mel *had* lied about his grandfather.

"Such an interesting country you have, mixed up by immigrants just like East Africa."

"The best," the ambassador said. "And we're hoping that our friend here"—he nodded toward Fong—"will accept the invitation of the American people and pay us a visit."

"I am sure he would be very happy to see your country," Fakhru said. In Swahili he said, "Three more cases of milk."

Fong felt his bladder bulge up into his rib cage and harden. It was odd. For the first time in his life he was in a place where he could not urinate at will. But he had made one hundred and twenty shillings, of which sixty was clear profit since the price of admission had to be deducted. The pain of his full bladder put these thoughts out of his mind. "Ask this *bwana* where is pissing," he grunted to Fakhru.

"If you please," said Fakhru, "can you direct my friend to the latrine?"

"To the *what*?"

"Latrine. He wants to peace."

The ambassador made a sour face, as if he had just swallowed something foul. He pointed to a doorway at the end of the hall and walked in the opposite direction, his face set in the same sourly bloated expression.

Fakhru led Fong to the toilet. "Here it is, American-style, *Wazungu choo*. Do not fall in."

Fong hopped inside and slammed the door.

Shoogra put her head into the hall and called Fakhru. She said it was almost midnight, time to go. The children were alone. She hinted that it was a bad hour to go back; the Africans who were getting drunk in the living room would start to leave any minute.

I have delivered the goods, thought Fakhru. He felt he had done his part. He had delivered Fong and also insured that he would stay by faking a deal and giving Fong the sixty shillings. Fakhru did not like the idea of leaving Fong alone; there was always the chance that, as Fong's interpreter, he could make more money. Alone, Fong would stay out of trouble, for he did not speak English, and none of the embassy staff spoke Swahili. There would not be any misunderstandings. Tomorrow would bring fresh profit, and the day after. Fong was the best bit of merchandise Fakhru had seen for a long time, and it struck him, there in the hallway ringing with Shoogra's unpleasant voice, that Fong was, in his own way, like the rest of the valuable goods, also from the black market.

Shoogra's voice was getting urgent. Fakhru told her to shut up, and, when she was silent, took a handful of peanuts from a plate and walked out to the van munching, his wife several steps behind.

Inside the toilet Fong looked at the large raised bowl. It looked like a Chinese vase, a fountain, nothing like the old familiar hole in the floor. His brain worked quickly. *How to do it?* He imagined various positions, but was not sure he would be on target. With his tongue between his teeth he climbed carefully on to the edge of the bowl where he stood, his feet on the rim, with one hand braced against the wall.

From his hiding place near the carving Mr. Chen watched the bathroom door. He had seen Fong enter. Minutes passed and Mr. Chen was seized with the fear that, for security reasons, Fong might be inside slashing his wrists. He looked around. There was no one in the hallway, but the laughter and loud singing inside was proof that he was not alone. Lifting the carving (it was of a man, slightly hydrocephalic, with popping eyes and an outstretched arm holding a spear; conveniently, it was almost life-size, or roughly Mr. Chen's height), Mr. Chen crouched behind it and held it before himself for camouflage as he picked his way down the hall to the bathroom.

He had ten feet to go when he heard:

"Oh, *there* you are. I bin lookin for you *every*place."

Mr. Chen spun round and tried to disguise himself as a feature of the carving.

Mel faced him, looked irritated and said, "I don't know what I'm gonna *do* with you, brother!" in mock motherly fashion, shaking his head.

Mr. Chen went stiff. He stared Mel in the eye. He contemplated leaping out the window, but there was no window in the hallway. Mel was holding a brandy snifter with an inch of brandy in it. Mr. Chen thought of dousing himself with Mel's brandy and setting himself alight (the whole embassy might go up with him), but he had not secured permission. It was enemy territory. The American stood and urged him. Now the American had him by the arm and was pulling him out from behind the carving. Mr. Chen kept his hand near the revolver strapped under his baggy woolen suit and followed Mel.

When Sam Fong came out of the toilet he entered a silent hallway. Fakhru was not there. Shoogra was gone. A large carving stood in the center of the floor. In the living room the noise had stopped. Fong saw only a large group of people with their back to him. He did not see that they were all drunk, that they were now drunk enough to speak and that they were speaking one at a time to Mr. Chen who stood at the center of the group as Fong had done. Unlike Fong, and perhaps because he was a diplomat, Mr. Chen had the good sense of timing to smile and say thank you when he was told that he, Sam Fong, was going to visit the United States of America free of charge, at the request of the American people.

Fong passed unnoticed through the front door of the embassy and went home. He told Soo of the evening, of the six sold crates and most of all of the odd gleaming fixture in the small closet. Before he went to bed he opened the door to the store and looked in. The stacks of milk crates, the cans of milk on the shelves, were silver in the moonlight that filtered through the shopwindow. There was a lot of milk; it nearly filled the store. But Fong knew it would be sold and he repeated this to Soo that very night.

# PART THREE

# 21

MR. CHEN COULD HAVE BEEN AN UNDERSIZED CLOTHES POST on which several thoughtless people had thrown a velour Tyrolean hat with a feather, a summer suit (so wrinkled and so large that it looked like two), a pre-knotted clip-on tie with the Washington Monument painted the length of it, two cameras and a tape recorder; the camera straps swung and everything bumped together as he walked. Mel Francey and Bert Newt carried the maps and brochures. They were deeply touched when the man they knew as Fong paused a few reverent moments before the Eternal Flame of the late President. They visited the Smithsonian Institution, the Pentagon where Mr. Chen tirelessly (and with special permission) snapped pictures; they stood before the stone gaze of Lincoln in his memorial, walked the wide avenues, chatted with some indignant sign-carrying mothers and youths with musical instruments who were picketing the White House; they drove to a small town in Maryland where not only Mr. Chen, but also Mel was refused service (Bert graciously said that it did not matter, he wasn't hungry anyway). In halting English Mr. Chen said he wanted to see everything and to collect information, street maps and postcards for his family album.

Four moon-faced Onondaga Indians were flown in from Syracuse, New York, to dance for him. Mr. Chen was delighted; he snapped pictures while the spools of the tape recorder turned slowly. After the dance Mr. Chen spoke with the Indians. He gave one of them his velour hat in return for a large, feathered headdress with tassels which he immediately put on. The oldest of the four, a man with squirrel pelts scarcely covering the soiled BVD's he wore beneath, refused to give Mr. Chen his tomahawk (Chen admired it) but made him an honorary chief of the Onondaga tribe. The old man said that if Mr. Chen ever happened to be in Syracuse he should give him a buzz. "I will if I can find one," said Chen. He did not know that he had made a joke until he saw Mel slapping his thigh and laughing. With the headline INJUNS FETE EX-RED IN D.C. POW-WOW (*"Just like a Filmshow," Says Chief Fong*) a picture showed Mr. Chen in his floppy warbonnet brandishing the old man's tomahawk.

He was denied nothing. For several weeks he lived with an American family in surburban New Jersey: he attended a church bazaar and cake sale with them, went to the local supermarket and marveled at the frozen foods, helped their teenaged daughter with her geography homework and in all ways shared the simple comfortable life of middle-class Americans. When Mr. Chen bade them farewell the man of the house said it would be a great thing indeed if people like Mr. Chen, whom he knew as Fong, foreigners and suchlike, could spend more time in the U.S.A. It was one pathway to understanding. "Foreign policy means people," the man said with emotion. And to this, Mr. Chen bowed. Later he visited high schools where he read to the assembled students a text prepared by Bert which began, "I have lived warmly with your people; I have seen your tremendous vitality; I have sampled your delicious hot dogs . . ." and ended "Now I know what it means to be an American. I have, just as a bold Italian from Genoa many centuries ago, discovered America." The speech was a huge success; it was quoted in scores of newspapers under the picture of the warbonneted Chen.

It occurred to Mel and Bert that Fong had learned a lot of English in a very short time, but they were not surprised. They said he must have known English all along, but as he gained confidence in the Americans and became less obstinate he had discovered that it was not necessary to hide himself behind the gibberish of Swahili.

Mel and Bert were given promotions even before their recording of the program that would tell the world with the speed of sound, better than any newspaper article, of the monstrous contradictions of Communism, of being a spy in East Africa and of seeing the Free World for the first time. From *Red-Handed*, the name of the program changed to *Red Tape, Red Herring, From Communist to Citizen* and *I Was A Menace*, to its final title, *Fong and the Indians*, subtitled *The Odyssey of a Communist*. This played up, as Mel put it, "Not only your Onondaga angle, but lots of other stuff as well . . ." The story, in three voices, was one of disenchantment, desertion and discovery: on a spying mission to East Africa, Sam Fong, a Chinese secret agent masquerading as a grocer, succeeds at finding out everything that the Americans are doing —the aim of his mission; but after bugging the American Embassy and sneaking around snapping pictures and generally casing the embassy buildings, he discovers, to his immense confusion, that Yankees are really nice people and mean well; he is so taken by their simplicity and good will that he refuses to relay his intelligence work to Peking. Having spied so thoroughly on the Americans he feels he knows them and understands them even better than he does his fellow Chinese, whom he has decided are worse than Nazis; and it is in the safety of this kindly embassy that he is granted asylum by two understanding and helpful information officers, Mr. M. Francey and Mr. B. G. Newt, Jr. He is quickly on a first-name basis (as he almost guessed he would be) with his new friends and he confesses that his one wish is to visit America. This, with the assistance of the American people and the staff of the American Embassy in East Africa, he does. Sitting in a Washington hotel room while four Onondaga Indians stamp on the floor and shake cans filled with beans, he discovers the rhythm and vitality of America, the meaning of freedom.

On a crisp fall day very recently this program was recorded. Mel Francey, Bert Newt and the man they knew as Sam Fong sat in a recording studio of the Voice of America and watched the minute hand of a noiseless clock bump toward twelve. "This is a dream come true," said Bert. Mel agreed; so did the man known as Sam Fong. In the program each man was to play himself, to relive the drama of those tense days in East Africa. The program was in three parts: *Africa, America, Awake*.

The first part opened with drumming.

Mel spoke first: "Africa! The *light* continent! Yes, in lightest Africa many new and wonderful things are happening every day of the year. Not the least of these is the heartwarming story of Fong and the Indians, the odyssey of a Communist, the awakening of Sam Fong, soon to become an American citizen . . ."

Then Fong: "I was born in the year 1918 of poor but honest parents in Central China. At this time the brutality of the vicious Communist thugs was snowballing into cold-blooded savagery. I did not know what to do. I was confused and beguiled by the new words on everyone's lips, and little did I know . . ."

Behind large glass windows engineers looked on and twirled knobs. The three men in the studio spoke in turn, with the knowledge that now everything was fine, aware that it had taken them all great trouble—even some misunderstanding—before this fulfillment came to pass. Now they were relaxed; it was clear that each of the three had succeeded in his mission and was very happy.

# 22

AND WHAT OF FAKHRU? HE HAD HEARD OF THE FONG-CHEN
mix-up the day after the embassy party from N. Bhikhu, the
travel agent who issued Mel, Bert and the man known as Sam
Fong the tickets. "You seem to be losing a tenant," said
Bhikhu. "I pray he is not jumping off your lease." Fakhru had
run to Fong's shop where he saw the Chinaman staring across
the counter at the canned milk on the shelves opposite. Fakhru
thought of going to the embassy to set the matter right but he
waited a day to reflect, and, after this reflection, decided that
it would be an error to do anything. Mel and Bert had gone
with their families; Bhikhu said they did not buy round-trip
tickets. They would not be back. The understanding that
Fakhru had reached with Mel and Bert did not extend to anyone else on the embassy staff. It would have been too much to
explain, and there was always the chance that it would back-
fire, that they would want their money back. The marketing of
Fong had taken place over many months with each move and
counter-move pushing the price up, increasing Fong's value,

adding the compulsion of mystery to the deal. During these months, and taking into consideration the airport business which made Fakhru a salaried consultant on Asian affairs in East Africa, Fakhru had managed to make, and save, a tidy sum. The American money had bought him Patel's dry goods shop and coffee *shamba*, Mehboob's paint store, several more *dukas* and a warehouse full of merchandise, all foreign. Taxes on imports were going up. He would only need to sit quietly on his merchandise. He was rich.

Being rich was the same as being poor except that he was now less busy. There was no work to do. Fakhru felt out of touch with his business; he had set it all in motion and now there was not only no need to keep pushing, but also no way of stopping it. This thought warmed him. He now used money where he had once used his wit. It was a chance to test proverbs. These he found false to the last; he had many good friends; he was able to intimidate anyone and buy almost anything, including love; and, contrary to the proverbs he knew, being rich pleased him—each digit to the left of the decimal point caused an added joy, a further refinement of happiness.

He missed Mel and Bert; this was his one sorrow. He missed being an interpreter for them, talking to them and turning their ignorance into money. The Americans were rich, earnest, harmless fellows and Fakhru felt it was a shame there were not more of them around. Life would be more pleasant with them. They would be trusting; they would leave important matters to people like himself; this would please everyone, even the Africans. African countries would tick over like General Motors. The British had done nothing except talk and make promises; when they tried to bargain they spoke in small figures. They were not honest, but they expected everyone else to be honest. The Americans were honest and assumed everyone else was honest. The British got nothing in return, deserved nothing; the Americans earned sympathy for their innocence, which was all they wanted. Fakhru no longer held the Americans' unbusinesslike attitude in contempt. They had made him rich.

There were the other Asians in East Africa. Most would

stay, some would be deported, none would leave of his own
accord: Fakhru knew this and there was never any need to
form an Asian political party in order to bully the Africans.
People were easy to buy; the Africans came cheapest of all.
As for the Asians—they ate regularly, arranged their mar-
riages, washed their feet, dressed well, bought cars, had
swamis and betel nut flow in; and there were enough women
for everyone. Business might be slack, but it would never
cease. There was unpleasantness, but in all the recrimination,
all the abuse, all the nastiness and accusation was the simple
truth—proved by the abuse—that the Asians were needed.
S. R. Patel's fear, that without persecution life was terrible,
may have been real but it was short-lived. A month after he
phrased his fear ("I feel like a transistor radio, nice and shiny,
new batteries, but . . . no programs, just wires inside . . .") the
Prime Minister viciously attacked the Asians, accused them of
being "big bosses, rich *bwanas* who pushing little poor countrymen all over the place . . ." Again Asians were openly
hated; they were called dirty dogs, hypocrites and bloodsuckers as before, and with this a vigorous knowledge of
identity was reborn in each Asian. Not protest—no one closed
his shop—rather, they felt pain, the sting which told them
they were alive, where and who they were; the abuse a re-
minder of their importance to East Africa. Not *bwanas* and
bloodsuckers, but indispensable. Business had not really
changed. Fakhru said that as he knew "the black mind," he
had expected a return of the abuse all along; the Africans
would keep talking and accusing, but they would never get rid
of the Asians. And even if they did, who would suffer? Only
Africans (and people like Gupta), who had never made a
shilling in their lives. Whether the Asians stayed or went elsewhere the Africans would be the only real losers. It was the
same with everyone who came to East Africa. The visitors and
immigrants seldom lost. For the Africans nothing would ever
change.

The State of Emergency had been a bad thing for business.
Everyone knew that. It was the Prime Minister's fault—all the
trouble. He was a cruel man, he wanted to be king (whose

idea was it to call him "The Supreme Redeemer"?), but he had good business sense. It was this that kept him in power. Fakhru understood him. With many other property-owners Fakhru feared the passing of the Prime Minister. "When the old man goes there will be trouble," Fakhru said at the close of business deals. The Asian answer, delivered with a jerk of the head and the exploded consonant, was inevitably, "Yes, please." But the deal had been closed and the money had changed hands, and that was the point of it all.

Fakhru sat in his office, comforted by the portrait of His Highness the Aga Khan. He picked up a thick pair of cutting shears and trimmed a betel nut. There were certainties, few, but important ones. The Asians were lost. The Africans did not matter. The British belched lies. The disorder and inconvenience of Africa killed charity and made profit possible. Fong still lived down the street. He owed. He had been used, but he was unworn, unsold. The Americans would stay; Africa was their green worm which, in all the childish innocence that their earnest stupidity was made up of, they valued more than treasure. The betel nut lay in slices on a white dish. Fakhru rubbed one smooth slice with his thumb and then placed the spotted nut slice on his protruding tongue. He smiled. Fong was still his.

# 23

SAM FONG COUNTED THE CANS OF MILK AND SHOUTED numbers to Soo who sat on her stool with the abacus on her lap. The filled shelves, the crates stacked near the counter, gave the store a look of prosperity; made Fong—with merchandise all around him—seem more a shopowner than ever. Six crates were stacked in the corner, awaiting delivery to the Americans. It was now only a week since the embassy party and Fong had seen Fakhru only once; he had bowed to Fakhru and not said anything. The two Americans had not been in the store at all. And just as well, Fong thought: he still owed money to Fakhru; the handbills advertising the American goods had brought no business. The retainer of ten shillings arrived every Monday; the debt to Fakhru was now over four hundred shillings. Fong did not want to speak to Fakhru or the Americans until he had orders to fill, or news, or money.

But there was no money. Fong's poverty was unchanged. Sales were small, in the smallest combination of large mocking coins which filled the biscuit tin but added up to very little. Soo threaded the pennies through their center holes; each heavy stack of twelve equaled one shilling. In the wooden box at the back of the store these threaded stacks of brown pennies looked like dog turds to Fong, reminders of his indignity.

Prices had gone up, rice was expensive and Fong had changed his diet. There were new foods, cheaper ones: sweet potatoes and peanut stew, boiled cassava and (it made him wince) bananas. They were all very recent to Fong; he had never tasted them before. Indeed, he associated their tastelessness with the dull sameness of life in Africa. The food was an indicator of why nothing had ever happened to the millions of East Africans: their country, their lives dominated by bananas. And now his own life as well. His loyalty to the Chinese diet, which had not flagged in thirty-five years in this strange land, was now at an end. Since opening the store things had altered a great deal for Fong, but now there was an almost explicit promise that nothing would change. He was certain of this when he looked at his plate. There was no rice on it. Locusts were heaped in a greasy mass next to a pale green lump of banana mush. Business could not worsen, but neither would it improve (the worst, the emergency, had already occurred and here he was, whole and unscarred by the events). There was the predictable weekly sum of ten shillings offset by the drabs of plugged pennies which did not equal ten shillings even at the end of the week. Except for the prayed-for derailment of the train there could be no more unexpected profits; he had attempted a swindle, but it had failed. So the change in diet, from Chinese to African, had come of necessity; once the necessity for it had been established there could be no argument. Resigned to bananas, Fong ate them in silence, with chopsticks. It was clear after a period of eating the local food that there was no going back. The immigrant's last compromise is his diet. He would stay in Africa and not starve; he was strong but there was not much time left; he knew he was closer to death than to China.

It was late in the evening. A beggar with tiny hands and large swollen feet crouched in front of the store waiting for

Fong to close. He wanted to curl up in the doorway for the night. He was patient. Fong looked at him. The beggar was black, homeless in his own country. Fong thought of the backroom, warm with the steady breath of Soo and the children. Fong would sleep soon and not be afraid. Africa did not frighten him: it was all accidental, and accidents could not be foreseen. The disordered slowness he knew existed in Africa was an assurance that the accidents would be small; he would not be harmed. He blew out the candle and locked the door. Even before he slid the bolt he heard the beggar fumbling with his rags, snorting, settling into position for the night.

Fong knelt in the darkness of the back room and said a prayer. Soo wheezed; outside, wild dogs were upsetting the trash cans and snarling. On the eaves bats squeaked like rusty wheels. Fong made the sign of the cross and then found his mat where he lay on his back, his hands folded across his chest, his face turned straight up. Just before he went to sleep Fong had several lucid thoughts, captions vivid enough to be dreams, but not grotesque, not peopled by demons in pursuit. Here he was in a foreign country, on a reed mat littered with dirt grains; he had lost his trade and had learned a new one, an uncomfortable, uncertain profession. But it had not been a plot against him; this was accident, not design. He was alive and old, with healthy children and a store full of merchandise which would be sold if God willed the derailment. He was an immigrant, a stranger, and yet had been treated no differently from anyone else. For this he was grateful. He had not been harmed, although he knew he was outnumbered by the Africans and outfoxed by the Indians. By nature men were different (the Chinese were the easiest of all to understand), but however much the differences created upset or alarm, still there could not be deliberate evil, for man was good. And it was sometimes a discomfort, though seldom a misfortune, to be far from home.

While Fong slept, a train chugged through the Rift Valley in a rainstorm three hundred miles from the store. The train clattered along, nosing through the unseasonable flood, its cowcatcher sending up huge streams of water to sizzle on its boiler. At two in the morning, near a village that was later to be widely photographed as the scene of rescue operations, tent hospitals and a wreckage of metal that was not cleared for months, the steam engine sagged on the unsupported tracks, the ties ripped away by the hillside torrent, and trembled in disjoined confusion down a gully. Its entire cargo of milk splashed out of the tank cars willy-nilly and mixed in puddles on the rain-sodden ground.

# About the Author

Paul Theroux is the internationally acclaimed author of such travel books as THE KINGDOM BY THE SEA, THE OLD PATAGONIAN EXPRESS and RIDING THE IRON ROOSTER, as well as a dozen novels, among them THE MOSQUITO COAST and O-ZONE. Theroux divides his time between London and Cape Cod.